Three Bullets

Gavin Jones

Gavin Jones

4/12/13

17:03

First published 2013
By Rowanvale Books
57, Brynllwchwr Road,
Loughor,
Swansea
SA4 6SQ
www.rowanvalebooks.com

A CIP catalogue record for this book is available from the
British Library.
ISBN: 978-1-909902-22-0

Three Bullets

Gavin Jones

For Donna, who kept that smile through the years I spent talking about writing this idea.

Love you.

TUESDAY: DAY 1

ONE

Can the dead think?

If they can he was dead.

How about senses? How long do they carry on for when you die?

One by one he set about testing them. He remembered reading somewhere that sight and touch were the last to go, so he tried the others first.

Hearing.

Something indistinct in the distance, a high pitched bleep – a lorry reversing, maybe.

Smell.

A hint of chemicals or disinfectant.

Sight.

Nothing.

Even with his eyes shut tight, something should have broken through the darkness. A flash of light. The coloured dots you see when you rub your eyes. At least an image projected from the brain.

There was nothing.

He felt his face; his sense of touch still worked. Some kind of damp material covered his eyes, not a great deal, just a slither, damp and stinking of a potent mixture of sweat and alcohol.

He ran his fingers along what felt like nylon bed sheets, the sheets gripped his legs like vines. He felt the vibrations from his pounding heart in his throat.

The coarseness of the pillow made it obvious this was not his bed. Recollections of the previous evening's events were sparce, and not helped by alcohol still being the dominant force in his bloodstream.

Through fear rather than choice, he suppressed a natural urge to cry out. He wanted to scream. He wanted to scream so loud and for so long that everyone would hear him and run to his aid, but muffled voices nearby made him feel uneasy.

He twisted his legs so they hung over the bedside; he listened for the voices, desperate for some idea of what to do next.

"See you later."

Someone was leaving. This was his chance. He dropped to the floor, cold against his bare feet.

Now he screamed.

Not for help, but out of pain; a fierce surge of pain that shot through his left hand like electricity. A sickening feeling pulsated in his stomach as metal pierced bone, a needle ripping through tender flesh.

He scanned his mind for memories of the previous night – still nothing. From the stench of his breath and the dryness of his throat he knew he must have consumed a hell of a lot more than his usual two pint limit.

As he hurried to escape, his blood-soaked hands left in their wake an abstract of scarlet lines across the gleaming floor, the white walls.

"Where do you think you're going?" called a lady's voice.

Panicked, he lashed out with a fist; the woman crashed against a door. He felt his way along a narrow corridor. His hands brushed across a large mushroom-shaped button, he pushed it and a cold breeze washed across his face as an electric door swished open.

There were footsteps; perhaps two more people, heading his way. He took one last breath and stepped forward. The momentum of weight shifted twice in seconds: a slow step forwards, followed by a thrust backwards as hands grabbed at his torso and dragged him back along the corridor. Between his panicked breaths he heard a mechanical hiss as the door he'd hope to escape through shut.

"Can you dress that wound?" said a man.

"It will need stitches," the woman replied.

He felt cold metal pushed roughly against his wrists. He expected the thin bones of his wrists to snap.

"No need for those," the woman said.

The pressure on his body was released for a second. He tried to resist but was easily forced back on to the bed.

TWO

In the struggle the blindfold had slipped, and blinding daylight now pierced his pupil.

Struggling as both strangers held him down, and becoming slowly accustomed to the sunshine, Daniel began to see the outline of three figures in front of him. A middle-aged lady holding a silver tray filled with medical equipment, and two men in dark suits, no ties. They looked particularly hostile.

"Make a habit of hitting women, do you Mr Stone?" said the older of the two men with a snarl, his tone deep and aggressive. "Would you like to press charges, Nurse Philpott?"

"No, it was an accident. I had no idea what I was —" Daniel began, his mouth dry.

"It's okay, something of an occupational hazard nowadays," the nurse interrupted, before turning to address her confused patient. "Mr. Stone, you are in Worcester hospital; you were admitted late last night with a few minor injuries but you are safe now," she continued, surprisingly unaffected by the swelling now blooming around her right eye.

From behind her, the blurred heads of other patients came into view as they scrambled to investigate the commotion for themselves. The hospital's security guard and the uniformed police constable loosened their grip on Daniel Stone.

"Minor injuries; wish we could say the same for the other one," commented the older man to whom Daniel took an instant dislike. "Take a break, PC Curry, we'll give you a shout when we're ready to go." He turned to Daniel. "I'm Detective Inspector Patrick Rhodes, and this is Detective Sergeant Joel Murray," he continued.

"We're here to ask you a few questions about how you sustained your injuries," said the second man, taking a seat next to the bed and flashing a Warrant card. "That is, if you're up to it?"

"This is a hospital? What sort of hospital *blindfolds* their patients?" shouted Daniel, pulling away from the nurse.

"The sort that doesn't want their patients getting infections in a scratched retina; we call it 'bandaging' rather than blindfolding. Blindfolding seems to get patients a little worked up," replied the nurse with a smile.

She pulled the curtains around the bed and started cleaning Daniel's hand, which he had laid back down so it could be readied for stitching.

"What happened to me?"

Daniel watched as the younger of the two policemen pulled his chair closer to the bed, turning it around so that he straddled it; he slouched forward, arms folded across the backrest.

"We were hoping *you* could fill in the details, Mr. Stone."

Daniel observed the pair for a few minutes; they were the stereotypical image of police partners. One strong and

6

aggressive – the one you feared; the other, younger, calmer, more approachable. Perhaps they'd been put together for that very reason. Daniel was unsure, but the combination worked, and worked well. He felt that his instinctive, intense dislike for one made him naturally more inclined to co-operate with the other.

Patrick Rhodes was well-built, fit, probably forty-five years old; from an era when police recruitment was height-restricted, he stood well over six feet tall. Daniel took him in: his eyes, two dark circles against a pale complexion, his hair somewhere between blonde and ginger, and in a style only celebrities and handsome men could pull off.

Daniel gazed now at the man's counterpart, Joel Murray.

He was easily two decades younger than Rhodes, average build, kept himself in shape. No doubt he was juggling anti-social hours and a demanding home life – Dan, having spotted the wedding band, figured the man was not long married. All in all, a life that allowed little spare time.

"How did I get here?"

"You don't remember?"

"No."

"A passerby found you last night, lying near the railway station," said Murray.

Daniel wasn't sure if it was the word 'station', or the metallic smell of blood, which drifted from the pink, pulsating mass of his open flesh-wound that cued his sudden recollection, but suddenly his mind spiralled off into fragmented flashback.

He was stepping onto a platform, leaving the train. He was about to call his son, like he did most nights. He dropped his mobile and as he fumbled beneath a bench for it, he was hit hard across the temple.

"I was mugged! They left me for dead," said Daniel.

The two policemen exchanged a knowing glance.

Daniel trembled as he recalled the mugging, every word deepening his pain.

Four, maybe five men had punched him, stamped on his face; he lay curled up, unable to defend himself against so many. He remembered being kicked around the floor. He faded in and out of consciousness, heaped there on the cold concrete of the platform. Salty tears ran from his chin as he listened to the tinny sound of his son calling out. The coldness of the platform, the warm trickle of blood that flowed from his nose, across his lips. How he eventually awoke from the blackout to the vile acidity of someone else's urine drying across his face and hair.

He lay exhausted, empty from the realisation of his attack, his gaze flitting between the nurse who continued to bandage his hand and the two policemen.

"Five men attacked you, left you for dead and you wake up here? You expect us to believe that?" Rhodes asked, his dark brown eyes glaring at Daniel, studying him, searching for the smallest sign of fear, the slightest flinch.

Rhodes spooked Daniel: the aggressive, cocksure stance, that deep, unforced tone.

"Yes," he answered.

"All done!" the nurse said. "Now, if you two can try and keep the intimidation down a little, I'll leave you to it."

"Maybe he needs a bit of intimidation. You've seen her, haven't you?" snapped Rhodes.

The nurse returned his glare before walking away, curtains flapping wildly in her wake.

"Just a broken nose, some bruised ribs and a scratched retina? Really? Only slight concussion from the unmerciful beating you describe? You're lucky to be alive, don't you think?" Rhodes asked, rapidly shooting the questions at Daniel.

Daniel turned his attention to the younger officer.

"Didn't you hear what I said? They beat me – one of them even pissed on me. I'd be dead if they hadn't been scared off."

"So there was someone else on the platform?" asked Murray.

A new image came into Daniel's mind: a plump, white-haired man in a stone-grey suit, black leather briefcase in one hand, semi-automatic pistol in the other. He'd waved the gun above his head, shouting and swearing, and through blurred vision Daniel watched as the stranger threw punches and kicks. Daniel felt an intense pain in his eye as one of the gang kicked him before racing away. Then everything went black.

"There was a man on the train, I got talking to him – he was the one that scared them off with a gun."

"A gun?"

The two policemen grinned at one another; they obviously knew more about this attack than they were letting on.

"Yeah, a gun. Why are you repeating everything I tell you?"

"Need to make sure you are one hundred percent certain of last night's events," said Rhodes, taking a peep through a gap in the faded blue curtains.

"Did this man have a name?"

Daniel noticed that every time Murray spoke he looked at Rhodes first, as if to get his unspoken approval.

"Jakub, his name was Jakub."

"A surname," snapped Rhodes.

"He was Czech I think... Tesar, yeah, it was Tesar; he was a salesman."

"Czech, like from the Czech Republic?" asked Rhodes.

"No, like from a bank!" Daniel snapped and watched the older officer's face redden.

"A salesman," said Murray, making a note of the name in a small notepad.

"Yeah, like I am." Daniel paused. A sinking feeling hit in a flash – in all the strangeness he'd forgotten he'd been sacked the previous day. "Like I was, until yesterday – I came back after two weeks' holiday and they'd been 'restructuring'. I gave them twelve years, they gave me twelve minutes," he continued, a tinge of sadness colouring his words.

"Mr. Stone, can you be sure of all this? I mean, you were *very* drunk when you were admitted."

"I had a drink or two, didn't know that was a crime. I'd just lost my job – I'd been expecting a promotion! This was the icing on the cake of a pretty shitty year."

"If it's okay with you, we need to get a member of our SOCO team down here to get some evidence."

"What evidence?"

Murray set about explaining to Daniel what was needed from him when the crime-scene officer arrived: a mouth swab, nail scrapings, maybe a few other things such as photographs of injuries.

Murray explained that all the items of clothing Daniel had been wearing when he was admitted had already been bagged and sealed for forensic tests. Each item was bagged separately in brown paper bags, sealed with Sellotape and identified with an exhibit label. All the time he talked, the young detective tried to make it sound as though giving this without a fuss would further help to eliminate him from any suspicion, making it sound comforting and sympathetic.

Daniel was also informed that an official statement would be taken a little later by a PC Amanda Wright, the uniformed officer who had travelled in the ambulance with him the night before from the scene. This wouldn't happen till PC Wright came back on shift at 2pm, and only after she had relieved PC Curry from his duties outside in the corridor.

"You could identify this Mr. Tesar?" asked Murray, switching his direction back to questioning.

"Of course; late fifties, light hair, nearly white, not much of it. He was fat, but only really around his stomach. The downfall of working on the road: service station lunches. He swore as well, I mean, like every other word. I don't like people like that; I feel it weakens what you have to say and makes you look stupid. Why? Do you think he can help?"

"Probably not, but we can't have salesmen running around with guns being all vigilante, now can we?" replied Rhodes, stepping around the side of the bed, taking hold of Daniel's bandaged hand and squeezing it hard against the metal frame of the bed, pinning it with his leg. There was a gasp of pain from the patient.

"Hey, Sir, no need for that," Murray said quietly, fearful of his superior.

Rhodes gave Murray a look that said in no uncertain terms: I'm in charge, now shut up. It worked.

It was clear to Daniel from the way Rhodes acted that Murray hadn't worked under him long, and was still getting to know what made him tick.

Daniel's face was red and contorted in pain and his breathing rapid as he tried to control the anger throbbing through his body. Distractedly, he watched Murray fidget in his chair. Then he noticed it, his savior: a four inch square piece of plastic with a circular orange button. Slamming his foot down on the button at exactly the same time as the alarm sounded, he let out a shriek.

"Listen, you piece of shit," said Rhodes, leaning in close. "I've heard enough. People like you repulse me – I've seen it a hundred times before: you keep up the convincing act of innocent victim when the real –" he broke off, releasing Daniel's hand as the nurse poked her head through the curtains.

"You okay, Mr. Stone?"

"Get them out of here!" He clasped his arm to try and ease the pain.

"Just going now anyway," said Murray, trying to calm the situation; he returned the chair and started to pull the curtains back.

Rhodes had other ideas; he leaned closer to Daniel's ear.

"Do you want me to tell you what I think?"

"I was the one attacked, remember – can't you see the pain I'm in here?"

"Come on you two, he's had enough!" said the nurse.

"Think of it this way, Mr. Stone: maybe this is as good as it's going to get from now on. You said there were four or five attackers, you and a gunman on that platform," Rhodes continued, oblivious to the nurse's plea for them to leave.

"Honestly, I've told you everything I remember."

"I'll jog your memory a little, shall I? My colleagues spent the majority of the morning watching CCTV footage

12

and there were only two people on that platform at the time of your so-called *attack*."

Confusion contorted Daniel's face as he struggled to prop himself up.

"You were one of those people, and the other was a nineteen-year-old girl. She's on life support now. So, you'd better start remembering – because you're looking at a *long* sentence if she doesn't pull through. Start thinking – and fast!"

*

Joel Murray pondered how to approach his boss with the question that had bothered him since leaving the hospital. He looked across at Patrick Rhodes, sat in the passenger seat. Murray fidgeted; he was warm.

"You seem distracted, boss."

"Just hungry."

"I'll stop somewhere, we can grab something."

Rhodes shook his head.

"Daniel Stone was not what I expected. What do you think?"

"I know what I think, Joel, but I'm going to hold on to my thoughts until I have evidence to back them up."

The car was filled with the sound of a phone ringing. Murray did not reconise the number.

"DS Murray."

"Joel. It's been a long time."

Joel instantly reconised the caller's voice. Richard West, Head Researcher for Midland News.

"Richard."

Rhodes gave Murray a look he did not like.

"Last time we spoke you were a week away from being transferred to that dive."

"That was eight months ago."

"Shit, that long? Time flies when you're investigating lost sheep."

"What do you want, Richard?"

"I need a favour. There's a rumour that your victim just died. Would you like comment on that?"

Rhodes pulled out his phone. There were no missed calls.

"You know that you need to go through the press office or speak to one of my superiors."

"Come on, Joel, mate - that would mean speaking to that prick Rhodes."

"Hi, Richard," Rhodes interjected.

Richard West paused just long enough to make it awkward.

"DI Rhodes, I hope you're looking after my friend Joel. Hope you're not teaching him any of your old policing habits."

"Every single one, except the one where I cut off an irritating little shit."

Rhodes leaned over and ended the call.

Murray smiled. The question he had about the manner of his interrogation no longer mattered. He was starting to understand what an influence Rhodes was going to be on his future.

"I'll call Roberts. We need to know if the girl is dead."

THREE

The sound of a heart rate monitor seldom brings feelings of joy. The high pitched blips and the silent pauses can hold someone's attention with so much intensity that it is hard to compare that quality of focus with anything else. In such a minuscule amount of time the emotional peaks and troughs can be extreme; almost a form of torture. The life of a loved one should never end to the discordant, computerised bleep of life support, to the sound of air draining, one last time, from a ventilator.

Sandra Flynn clutched her daughter's hand. She brushed a stray curl away from her daughter's brow; her daughter's fine, sun-kissed mane mostly the result of expensive hair extensions.

Sandra wept quietly, her tears falling freely onto the bed.

Greg Flynn leaned against the wall, his face drained, his eyes burrowing into the gleaming white and black check of the floor. Greg was tall and lean, despite his refusal to exercise and his appalling diet. It had been over eighteen hours since they'd awoken to a world they now struggled to make much sense of, desperately needing each other but unable to communicate, too busy trying to answer the questions that went off like firecrackers in their minds.

Barely held together by meters of plastic tubing, machinery and bandages, so delicate a life. The life of their nineteen-year-old daughter Abbie. Thick dressings hid the three-inch hole in her skull, made with such violent force that small fragments of bone had splintered into sections of her brain tissue. On the right hand side a second section of skull was missing, the result of a careful surgical procedure to relieve pressure on her swelling brain. Oblivious to the horror that surrounded her, she lay oddly at peace in the rigid shell of her near-lifeless body.

The silence suddenly gave way to Greg's loud sobs, his hard exterior all at once displaced by a memory. Closing his eyes, he buried his head in his hands and shook, as though trying to rid himself of the image.

"Greg."

"Abbie was about six, San - she fell from the slide, remember? Cut her knee badly, cried and cried for hours."

"I remember, at the park."

"I told her. I told her I would fix it. I would make sure she never got hurt again!" he sobbed now, unable to compose himself.

Sandra placed her head back on the bed, nestling against Abbie's leg.

"She asked me to promise because *I* never broke a promise. I haven't kept my promise now though, have I?" he asked, pointing uselessly to his daughter. "If I find out who did this – I will kill them! That's one promise I *will* keep! Oh, my beautiful, beautiful little girl."

The room fell silent once more but for the mechanical noises. Mrs. Flynn rubbed her daughter's arm tenderly. Her gaze fixed, she did not look up even as her husband ferreted about in the pockets of his black overcoat.

"I'm going for a coffee. You want one?"

"No, thank you. Why don't you drink it outside, in the car park – get some fresh air, take your phone, ring your mom, she'll be worried."

She hated the way he drank coffee, slurping it until it was all gone before it had even had cooled; it annoyed her beyond belief. One of those things she'd never told him. Oh, now and then she made a weighted remark: "You in a rush, asbestos throat?" Now just the thought of his slurps echoing around the room might easily see her blurt out years of untold annoyance.

Once out in the corridor, Greg was stunned by the noise. No-one here sat in silence; they rushed around, carrying on with the business of ordinary life.

Next to Abbie's room, an empty chair rested against the wall; PC John Hill had been sitting in it most of the morning. Greg put on his coat, pulling the collar tight around his neck, before drifting along the corridor. Though there was no need for a coat, Greg felt cold to the bone. Head down, counting the change that rattled in his shaking hand, he avoided making eye contact with anyone; a desperate attempt to not witness people's everyday actions. Doing so would have meant acknowledging that his daughter's life was a mere insignificance; a life that filled his own heart with so much warmth was just another half-smudged surname on a hospital white board.

Coins clattered to the tarmac in all directions; some rolled, a few span, most just lay there in the aftermath of an accidental collision.

A weary-looking man stood above Greg Flynn, looking down at him as he rushed to pick up the scattered money.

The man was dressed in a tatty and faded blue hospital gown, a pair of white Nike trainers sparkling beneath. White material, a dressing, covered the man's left eye, and a bandaged hand poked from his left sleeve.

"Sorry," said the man.

"I should have been looking where I was going," Greg replied before standing up, pushing past the stranger and walking away.

*

The brand new trainers squeaked, their laces dragging along the floor as Daniel wearily crept toward Abbie Flynn's room. The shoes were, along with a few other items, new. Nurse Philpott had been kind enough to fetch them during her break.

His hand trembled as he gently pushed the silver door handle; no click, no squeak. He paused. This was wrong, it was sick, an intrusion on another human's private grief, but he had to see her. A quick glance might give him some clue as to what had happened on the platform the night before. A peek couldn't hurt anyone – from the way the detectives had described her, she was probably unconscious. Of course, this didn't make it right, just easier.

FOUR

Once in the room he reeled backwards – he reached for the wall to stop him falling. His lungs worked overtime to keep up with his need for breath. Daniel glanced at the girl's mother, not wanting to see, but unable to look away – she was asleep at her dying daughter's side; his eyes traced too the pipes and tubes that disappeared beneath the girl's blanket. Minutes passed as he took the scene in, watching the ventilator rise and fall.

Despite the confusion of pipes entering the girl's mouth and nose and the intense swelling of her face, Daniel knew one thing: he did not recognize her.

Besides, there was no way he could have done what the police were accusing him of. Relief spread through his body, only seconds later being replaced by the realisation of his actions. His stomach churned. He heaved, half covering his mouth. Gripping the door handle he went to leave, but, through a gap in the half-closed window blinds, he caught sight of a man approaching the room. It was the man he'd bumped into before. Daniel held the handle tight as this same man now gripped the other side. Daniel's grip tightened as he struggled to keep the door from opening.

"Mr. Flynn, there's an Edna on the phone. Apparently you left a message on her answer-machine."

The pressure on the handle eased. Across the room the girl's mother began to stir; she lifted her head from the bed, turning to look at the door, which closed with a swish.

Vomit splattered the floor. The stark brightness of the corridor and the rush of adrenaline were all too much for him, that his repulsion at what he'd done. Sneaking into people's rooms; what was he doing? A second wave of vomit exploded up the wall as he dropped to his knees. He closed his eyes. Two nurses ran past him and into another nearby room.

"Can someone get this drunk out of here?" a female doctor shouted.

Greg paced back along the corridor, took a quick look at the grounded man, and pushed the door to his daughter's room open.

"Mr. Flynn, I was just coming to speak to you," the female doctor called.

"Can you give me a second? I'll be back out in a moment."

"May I come in and speak to you and your wife?"

"I'd rather hear the news first, before she finds out. I'd rather break it to her." Greg disappeared into the room.

The doctor glanced down at Daniel, who was clutching his abdomen, then turned back along the hallway to shout for a nurse.

"The state of the NHS in this county is a joke, there's some poor bastard walking about in a hospital gown with trainers on, stinking of piss and throwing up out there, and no-one is doing anything about it. He's got a patch on as well, like some sea-sick pirate."

Greg placed a cup of coffee on the side by his wife. "Bought you a coffee in case you fancied one. It's really nice, to be honest, wasn't expecting it to be, they just need to make the cups bigger – didn't last five seconds. Just got to pop back out for a second."

"Greg, did you come back a little earlier? I swear someone else was in here," asked his wife.

Greg gave no answer; he had more pressing business back in the corridor.

Once outside Greg spoke to the doctor, his heart beating hard in anticipation of bad news.

"Would you like to go to a quiet room, Mr. Flynn?"

"Just tell me here! Please cut all the crap out, just tell me how it is, and without the medical jargon."

The doctor flicked through a pile of papers she was holding. The man in the corridor slid a little closer, his head still in his hands.

"Mr. Flynn, from your daughter's injuries it's obvious she was involved in a rather vicious attack. We have worked hard to release the pressure on her brain; we are unsure at the moment what, if any damage has been done. She's not breathing independently, and there could be some issue with messages from the brain to the rest of the body. We've done some tests, which rule out sexual assault."

Greg looked the doctor full in the eyes and smiled. He didn't speak, but the doctor could see he was trying to say 'thank you'.

"Abbie does have a four-inch gash at the back of her knee, which has severely damaged the cartilage and tendons, and the kneecap is detached. We are preparing for surgery to repair the knee, which could mean taking a skin graft from her right thigh. Mr. Flynn, we're trying our best to stabilize your daughter. We hope for a positive conclusion; however, you and your family need to be aware that she is extremely ill and there is still a possibility her body might not respond. The next twenty-four hours are critical to her recovery."

Greg just nodded his head. She had made it as clear has he could have hoped for, and there was no more to be said.

*

Another stream of sick flowed from Daniel's mouth as the description of the girl's injuries sank in.

"Will someone please come and sort this mess out!" the doctor called.

"Mr. Stone, what are you doing down here?" said the nurse who had stitched Daniel's hand as she ran past. She took hold of him, pulling him to his feet, and started to walk him away from the room.

"Ruined your lovely gown I see – glad we use an outside laundry service!" she laughed.

Daniel watched Mr. Flynn – the girl's father he supposed – and the doctor continued their conversation.

"There's someone upstairs waiting to see you."

"Who?"

"Don't worry, not police this time."

The pair entered a lift. Nurse Philpott pushed the number two button and waited for the door to close.

Daniel caught a glimpse of a face in the thin mirror on the side of the lift. He recognised the face no more than that of the girl lying like a corpse. His bruising and slight swelling to his nose gave a warped shape and perspective that he did not like. He very rarely spent long looking in the mirror, but now he was drawn to inspect each pore, each unshaven hair, each blemish, hoping that doing so would spark off some needed comfort.

"What were you doing down there? That policeman has been down here all day; you'd be in serious trouble if he saw you."

"I was looking for the truth. I watched the policeman leave! I'm not stupid!"

"Listen, you've had a heavy knock to the head. My advice is to go home, rest and the truth will probably find you."

The lift jolted and the door slid open. The smell of freshly-brewed coffee drifted to Daniel's nose from a franchise shop in the atrium of the hospital. The bright hospital entrance was all glass and plastic trees. The nurse escorted Daniel toward the exit, where the scent of coffee was replaced by the acrid stench of cigarette smoke. Daniel smiled as a young boy ran toward him, his arms outstretched. The boy came to a rough halt as he crashed into Daniel's stomach and they embraced.

"What happened, Dad?"

"Just an accident mate, I'll be fine," Daniel replied, rubbing his son's spiked brown hair.

"You heard 'bout Max Flynn's sister?"

"No, son," said Daniel.

He looked down at his son as they walked through exit doors. Everything was going to be fine, this was what he needed: approval from his son, reassurance that he was a nice person. Not a person capable of producing the horror that had befallen that girl.

Once outside in the warm April sun, Daniel spotted his ex-wife Natalie sitting in the passenger seat of a large black BMW X6. He recognised the man sitting in the driver's seat.

Tom Gibbs, husband number two – the sickliest, most perfect example of man that God had ever deigned to gift the world with. There was no end to his exceptional qualities: tall, handsome, rich, generous and seven years Daniel's junior.

What Daniel hated more than anything else was that he actually liked Tom, really liked him, and couldn't say a bad word about him. This grated – surely he was supposed to hate this man, the man who'd married the love of his life.

"Didn't know your mom cared so much," said Daniel.

"It was Tom's idea," explained his son with a forced smile. "Max Flynn, he's in my year at school!"

"Sorry, I don't know him. Tom got a new car?" replied Daniel his eyes fixed on the sparkling alloy wheels of the luxury vehicle.

"Yeah, he bought Mom a white one. Villa gave him a new deal. Dad! Max's sister Abbie got beaten up last night, she's proper bad, and he wasn't in school today. Jamie reckons she's going to die because her brain actually came right out of her head!"

"Ollie, that's not a nice thing to say. I'm sure she'll be fine. You shouldn't listen to silly rumours."

The boy frowned before running to the car and kissing his mother on the cheek.

"I'll be back in two hours, if that's okay?" Natalie Gibbs asked her son. He nodded and she flashed a quick smile toward her ex-husband as the car pulled away in near silence.

WEDNESDAY: DAY 2

FIVE

The smeared and grubby window of the Station Bridge pub was the perfect front row seat from which to view the crime scene without actually standing beyond the blue and white police tape. The dreary square structure towered above all the other buildings, casting an ominous shadow over the crime scene. It was far enough away for the police officer who'd been standing guard all morning not to suspect anything, and just close enough to observe all the comings and goings of the investigation. On a good day the Station Bridge could have up to ten drinkers, all engaged in rowdy conversation. Today was not a good day. The proximity of the police had scared the regulars off; the manager, Mark Cavendish, might turn a blind eye to the odd bit of weed and counterfeit CDs being sold, but naturally the police tended to have other ideas.

Tammy Cavendish, the peroxide-blonde, tangerine-skinned manager's daughter and lone barmaid, had only two customers. A skinhead man in his late twenties slouched on a ripped leather bar stool; a Wolves Football Club tattoo poked from under the sleeve of his tight t-shirt, showing his toned muscular arms off. His nose had clearly been broken and reset many times – a few times too many. If he had looked up then he'd have noticed the barmaid trying to attract his attention, but he was far too engrossed in his fourth pint of the day to be bothered with her. He knocked the remains back and pushed the glass along the bar toward the girl.

"I'll have another," he said, fumbling in his wallet for change.

A plastic card slipped from the safety of the leather and flew across the bar. Tammy sauntered over and picked up off the floor, reading it aloud.

"Alex Burns, A2B Taxis. Well, I'll have to remember your number. I would love you to take me home after a girly night out in Worcester."

Alex ignored her attempts at flirting. Instead, he slipped the card back into his wallet and handed over a ten pound note for the drink she'd finally begun to pour.

"Not working today then? Shame that – I could have done with a lift to the hairdressers later, need to get a new style – not had it done for weeks," she said.

"Not on till ten tonight."

"Haven't you had too much to drink to be driving?"

"I'll be okay by then."

With that, Alex stood up and stumbled over to a comfy sofa near the pool table, putting his feet up on a chair to watch the cricket.

Across the pub, the greasy head of Colin Templeton rested against the glass. Eyes wide, he scanned the disruption outside. A police community support officer struggled to keep control of a growing number of nosy onlookers. Among the crowd were a few local journalists, hanging around hoping for a glint of breaking news. They should have known better. A press office had been set up and all the information the police had *chosen* to disclose had already been released.

Colin sat in a stained chair which creaked as he sipped at the now flat Coke he'd ordered over two hours ago. Colin loved crime, especially gruesome crime, which rarely happened locally. Usually, Colin had to make do with his ever-growing collection of *CSI*, *Morse* and horror DVDs.

He wore a black T-shirt emblazoned with an image of a snake emerging through the left eye-socket of a skull. The shirt was faded where his pot belly jutted out; he also wore dirty stonewashed jeans. His un-styled hair and lack of facial grooming made him look at least ten years older than his actual age of forty.

He twisted his head to gawp at the barmaid's cleavage, which struggled to stay in her low-cut blouse as she leaned against the bar, reading a copy of *Heat* while simultaneously managing to tap away at her iPhone.

"I'll give you a ride," Colin said, drooling slightly.

"What you say – you dirty perv?" Tammy snapped back, before disappearing behind her magazine once more.

"To the *hairdressers* – you silly little girl! I'm a taxi driver. Booked the day off so I could watch this." He pointed out the window. "But I would rather watch you, eh, sorry, *help* you out," his said, his voice croaking with nervous anticipation.

At the sound of a car accelerating Colin snapped his attention back to the window. The road was still closed to traffic coming down the hill, so this had to be someone important arriving at the scene.

"Oh, Billy big bollocks is here, now the real fun begins," he muttered, as a silver Audi A4 pulled up and DI Patrick Rhodes sprang from the driver's side.

Suddenly, Colin's concentration was broken by his vibrating phone. He checked the display, which read 'The Bitch'.

"What you want?" he said. "Yeah...yeah...just out...in a bit... I don't know... I'll do it when I get back... I don't know... Well it's not my fault you've shit yourself... I'll have to change your sheets...yeah and your stinking piss bag... For God's sake, Mother, I don't know... Yeah, I'll get your fags." He hung up and grumpily shoved the phone into his pocket.

Now he was angry. Here he was, had taken a day off work for this, and he'd missed watching Rhodes, who was now well beyond the cordon and completely out of sight.

"You fucking bitch, I've missed it now!" Colin stormed, slamming the half-full glass of Coke on the bar and heading for the door.

"Hey weirdo! You've left your paper!" Tammy called after him.

"You should watch your mouth, young lady. Another thing you should watch is your face when you're doing your slap. It's not a colouring book, love! Ease up a bit, yeah?"

"Arsehole."

"Talk to the wrong person that way and you might end up like the girl they found out there."

He snatched his copy of the *Express* and *Star*, which was, coincidently, opened at a page showing a smiling Abbie Flynn, before storming out of the pub, making sure to slam the large double doors as he did so.

SIX

The station was nothing fancy. Recently refurbished, it had a few new touches. On the town side of the track sat a small brick-built ticket office that housed three counters, two information screens and a tiny retail kiosk. There was a cashpoint and a self-service ticket machine on the outside wall. A set of wooden doors led passengers to the northbound platform. The platform consisted of a thirty-foot piece of concrete that sloped down to track at either end. There was a roofed footbridge three-quarters of the way down that led to the slightly less sparse southbound side.

This piece of concrete was similar in length, and had a shelter made of metal. The shelter was home to some of the town's wisest words, etched into the Perspex windows.

There was also a ramp, that lead back to the main road. At the bottom of the ramp leading to platform two, DI Rhodes stood talking to uniformed constable Rob Jones; both now wore thin, blue-paper overclothes and plastic overshoes.

A man, decked out in a white plastic boiler suit and shoes, crawled on hands and knees along the edge of the platform that led to a shallow, shrubby area.

As quickly it had appeared, a flash of green and white disappeared: the London–Midland thundered through the station, sounding its horn.

"It's not going great, Sir. We have four officers doing shop enquires and three doing houses but we've hit a wall as far as anything solid's concerned," the constable explained.

"You can't get any more solid than a wall," Rhodes said, laughing.

"No-one wants to communicate with us, Sir."

"Very PC of you, Jones; you mean no-one *can* communicate with us. We all know that this whole area is predominately eastern-European now."

"There are a few Polish around here, Sir, but not as many as people believe."

"A few? There's far more than a few. How many towns the size of Kidderminster do you know that have *eight* Polish supermarkets and even a Polish restaurant? Not very many, I'll bet. Then there's the Latvians, Lithuanians – and the rest! Can we not get Marek to help out on this one?" Rhodes continued as the pair walked back up the ramp toward the street.

"He's back in Poland this week – returns next Tuesday."

"Not a great time for him to go on holiday."

"His dad died."

"Then it's not a great time for his dad to die."

The Alpha Oscar 1 helicopter soared above their heads carrying out aerial photography and video recordings of the area.

Rhodes stopped at the street, removing his overclothes and taking another look at the century old steel bridge. It was painted with a multitude of colours that spelled out the word KIDDERMINSTER, a welcome symbol to tourists. The unmistakable smear of dark dried blood just below the letter M was far less welcoming. His eyes followed the curb to a damaged lamp-post; he continued making mental notes detailing his surroundings.

"Come and take a look down there," he said. "I count over thirty shops and a pub, and there's another pub out of view around the corner. Of those thirty shops, at least twelve are take-aways. So that's at least fourteen establishments that were open, and, more importantly, still had custom when this attack took place. Ten o'clock on a Monday night is not peak time but there should still have been enough people around to have seen something." Rhodes shook his head. "It took six minutes between them leaving the train platform to the initial 999. This is a busy road, Jones, someone had to be about."

Something wasn't right; he'd been a detective too long to believe that Daniel Stone had been responsible for the attack on Abbie Flynn. Nothing was that cut and dried. And even if he had done it, someone must have seen something. He would need some tangible evidence if he was to charge Stone.

"We need to get officers concentrating on the retail CCTV; we have further information that a gang of at least four youths, probably all male, were in the area and heading away from the station around that time. If we can identify this gang and eliminate them this will lead us back to our only significant witness."

The detective ducked under the police tape and signed a clipboard that a PCSO held out to him.

"Check opening times – some of the Chineses don't open Monday," he called back to PC Jones. He crossed the road and pushed the door of the Station Bridge wide open before vanishing inside.

It had been over seven years since he had entered this particular establishment, and that had been for business rather than pleasure. Christmas Day 2007, he'd been called to an incident: the licensee had been bottled by a customer he'd refused to serve. The decor was awful then and wasn't much better now. It still smelt as bad; the sweet musky smell of stale beer that made the carpet sticky.

Rhodes liked it, and though he would never chose to drink here, it had the exact appearance he felt a pub should. He hated those franchises, tacky recreations of old country-style inns, everything decked out in polished oak, spotlights sunk into the fake beamed ceilings, the focal point a grand log fire with its fake glow in line with Health and Safety regulations. They'd spend all that money only to promote their cheap, two-for-one meal deals and drinks promotions to get punters through the door.

"Can I speak to Mark Cavendish, please?" he said loudly, so as to be heard over the blaring Amy Winehouse song.

"Isn't up," Tammy replied, without even lifting her eyes from her phone.

"Is he here?"

"I said he ain't…"

"I'm not deaf, Miss. I am, however, a bit tired – give him a shout, tell him that DI Rhodes, Kidderminster CID, is waiting *impatiently* by the bar."

On overhearing this, Alex Burns sank further into his seat.

Tammy went to answer back, but on seeing Rhodes's expression, changed her mind.

"I'll go get him."

"Thank you," Rhodes couldn't help adding. One of his worst habits, that, his need to get the last word in, especially when dealing with a disrespectful teenager.

Rhodes walked around, taking in all the pub had to offer. He looked out of the window where Templeton had sat earlier, the glass still smeared with Templeton's grease. After making a quick note of what could be seen from the window, he examined the rest of the pub. He found it strange that, while the furniture looked as though it had been there since the First World War, there were thousands of pounds worth of entertainment equipment knocking about. Not only were there five fifty-inch flat-screens, a large projection screen, a top-of-the-range sound system and karaoke machine, but on a board behind the bar a list of all the 3D football matches that the pub would show.

"Better be good," said the giant of a man now standing behind the bar.

Cavendish was about six-foot-five and nearly as wide, Rhodes reckoned. His shining, hairless head covered in tattoos, the man didn't look as though he needed help throwing troublemakers out. Rhodes realised why he hadn't been called out to this pub since Cavendish had taken over.

"You must be Mark Cavendish. You're not what I was expecting."

"Don't tell me – you were expecting me to be riding a bike?"

"Heard it before, have you?"

"Once or twice."

"I'm DI Rhodes. I'm here to ask you a few questions about the incident that took place at the station on Monday night."

"I saw nothing, me man. Now, if you don't mind, I've got things to do."

Rhodes noted how soft Cavendish's Black Country accent was. It was an accent that normally sounded harsh in the detective's experience, but Cavendish's tone was unusually warm.

The other oddity was the lack of swearing. Rhodes had expected at least two or three expletives from a man who'd personally chosen to decorate his head with pictures of dragons and knives, a man who spent his working day in the presence of drunks.

"So you're saying that no-one in here last night saw a thing. You were open?"

"We was. I was working. Quiz night, so loads of us were in here. However, no-one leaves quiz night until it finished; there's a four pint pitcher for the winners."

"You got an issue if I ask a few of your punters some questions?"

"Yeah, actually I have. You won't get any info from the guys that come in here."

"And why's that?"

"Firstly, there isn't anyone here is there? You friends out there have seen to that."

"Maybe that hot taxi driver round in the pool area can help!" Tammy interrupted.

Rhodes peered around the corner. There was no-one there, just a half-empty pint glass.

"See, he's done a runner as well," said Mark. "Secondly, you're *the filth*."

"I think the fact that two local people have been attacked might sway people's opinions."

"I ain't so sure of that meself. You see, I've been done over five times in three years and you weren't so quick knocking on me door then! After the first one, I dealt with it me own way."

"Insurance paid out though." Rhodes flicked his eyes up to the big screen, making sure the manager noticed.

"All my own money," Cavendish said, before walking off.

"I only have a few questions, but probably better if I pop back later when you're a little busier?"

"I tell you what, why don't you *not* come back and I'll ask around; if I hear anything you'll be the first to know," Cavendish called back down the hall.

"I'd rather ask them myself. You might not ask the right questions."

Again, Rhodes had had the last word, which made him feel happy, even if that meant he was now standing alone in the bar, his feet stuck to the filthy carpet.

THURSDAY: DAY 3

SEVEN

Patrick Rhodes's jagged, bitten nails raked at the tender reddening skin on his shins. The mixture of pain and relief made it hard for him to stop even though blood seeped like volcanic lava down his eczema ridden legs. He didn't mind the sight of blood; he knew police officers that couldn't stand it, even paramedics that hated the stuff, and surgeons, too, that found it repulsive.

For Patrick it wasn't an issue, just part of the job. He knew sales analysts who hated numbers and fishermen who got sea-sick; it didn't make them any less competent. He dealt with the human chardonnay quite a lot: on one occasion he'd even lain watching a couple of pints of his own precious blood free itself from his radial artery. The result of acting first on a call out and thinking about the consequences much too late. The sight of his own blood had given him a twinge of pleasure ever since. Not a sick, twisted feeling, just an awareness that he was still alive, and as it started to clot and dry he knew he would be okay for a little while longer.

Stress was what the doctor believed was behind this, his most recent flare-up of eczema. He'd laughed out loud as the doctor scribbled out another prescription for some useless steroid cream. Another tenner wasted. This latest purchase would be quite at home with all the other creams, sachets of Dioralyte and flu remedies in the Quality Street tin in the kitchen cupboard.

Stress didn't affect men like Rhodes: twenty-five years in the police force (twenty of those spent working his way up through detective ranks) had taught him how to *deal* with his emotions.

A senior officer had once told him that the best way to cope was to leave it all at work – to never take the job home. He had disagreed. In his opinion a good detective should eat, sleep and breathe each new case he or she worked on, immersing themselves in the finer details.

Patrick Rhodes was an expert at diving deep into a crime, deep into the minds of his suspects, and sometimes into the minds of their victims too – if necessary. He prided himself on remaining unmoved, allowing nothing to cloud his judgment.

Some of the images he'd witnessed throughout his career would terrify even the most fortified mind. He saw again the decapitated three-year-old boy who'd been hit by a motorbike. The number of drownings he'd been called to, the bloated bodies. Young girls affected him worst. A little too close to home, and now the image of Abbie Flynn's battered visage haunted his mind.

This had happened to him only once before: the Sarah Allen case.

A twelve-year-old girl who'd murdered a sixteen-year-old boy outside of her school; she'd used a kitchen knife hidden in her clarinet case. Rhodes interviewed her and, for the longest time after could not erase the image of her petrified eyes; that face had haunted his dreams. He knew she'd committed the crime but never figured out why. He'd been convinced someone else was behind it. However, as a newly-promoted sergeant he found it difficult to convince anyone else. The real culprit went free while Sarah Allen rotted in jail.

He held a tatty photograph tight between his thumb and index finger, turned at an angle, illuminated by the light of his muted television. The television stand leaned against the wall and floor, a constant reminder of the ever-growing list of jobs he had still to complete some two weeks after he'd moved.

A young girl smiled back at him, her face beaming with joy, her arms draped around a large German Shepherd puppy. Rhodes glanced at his watch: 4.06am. In four hours he'd be back at his desk, looking at the pictures of Abbie Flynn that now decorated the incident room. One of them showed the victim before her attack, her smile not unlike his daughter's smile, here in this picture he held so dear.

He shuddered.

A line of blood from underneath his nails smeared the girl's face. The next few minutes passed in a daze as the policeman struggled with harrowing images that bombarded his mind. Images of his Sadie, face down on that same road near the railway; him rushing to her side, turning her over and recoiling at the sight of her pummeled face.

The bathroom light flickered on. Rhodes began to bathe his legs with a flannel, trying not to make too much noise, not wanting to disturb his still-sleeping wife. Fumbling past the toothpaste and deodorants in the cabinet, his hand stretched right to the back, just behind two half-used canisters of shaving foam. There he found his 'emergency cigarette' – a little damper than when he'd hidden it, but still okay to smoke.

Remembering to miss the creaky third-but-last step, Rhodes tiptoed down the stairs, turning the key on the back door.

Since the age of fourteen he'd been a smoker, and was unsure just how many days, months, even years, he'd been in the early stages of quitting, or even just *thinking* about giving up. He knew this figure out numbered the amount of time he'd smoked, so he was, as always, quick to praise himself for at least trying.

It had been three weeks, four days, twelve hours and three minutes since his last drag – not that he had been counting. He closed his eyes and exhaled with pleasure. The woody, almost earthy smell filled his nostrils.

His eyes heavy and sore, he gazed along the dark rooftops that sloped down the hillside from the end of his new back garden, giving him the ideal vantage point from which to view the town. Even at this time in the morning it was lit up, still showing signs of nightlife. He took one last lingering drag before tossing the nub into a metal bucket.

It didn't take long for him to get dressed. He still hadn't found the time to build the new wardrobe so his clothes lay across the bed in the spare room, along with all the other unpacked boxes.

He kissed his wife and whispered, "Love you."

He drove the short distance to the police station.

From the moment of that farewell kiss to turning off his engine took a total of twelve minutes. He scrolled through the contact list of his personal Blackberry, still unsure why he had come to work so early. Now and again his thumb hovered over the entry marked SADIE. Rhodes dialed the number but hung up before the call connected.

He just wanted to speak to her, to make sure she was okay; of course, he knew she was fine. She was always fine, but after what had happened to Abbie Flynn he wanted make sure.

6:03am. Maybe give it an hour – he knew what she'd be like if he woke her at this hour.

*

Across town another man couldn't sleep.

Daniel Stone popped two yellow and red capsules in his mouth, swallowed and tightened his lips.

Holding his good hand down with the other, he tried, in desperation, to stop it from shaking.

Resting against the cold kitchen work surface he emptied the contents of his glass down the steel sink and watched as it spiraled around the plug hole. The sun began to creep   through the kitchen window, finding its way through the ever-widening gaps in the ageing fence at the end of his garden.

Daniel watched a blackbird as it hopped across the lawn and started to play tug-of-war with the soil, using a plump worm as his rope. The blackbird won - his prize was to sit and rip at the soil-filled guts.

Daniel vomited again and again.

EIGHT

Clutching a half-eaten bacon and mushroom sandwich smothered in brown sauce in one hand and a newspaper in the other, Joel Murray strode, full of confidence, into the CID office. He looked more like he was going to a wedding than spending a day at work. He wore a stylish navy suit, a crisp white shirt and a navy and white striped tie.

"You shit the bed or something?" he said, ribbing DI Rhodes who was sitting at a desk covered in that morning's newspapers. Near him were detectives DS Jackie Roberts and DC Glenn Bates.

"Something like that," Rhodes replied.

"How can you eat that crap every day?" asked DS Roberts.

"Rather easily, what's wrong, does it not get the approval of a Special K girl?" said Murray.

"Contrary to male ignorance, not all women eat, or actually even like, Special K."

Just then, a young, short and extremely inexperienced detective crossed the office, carrying a tray. He proceeded to hand out hot drinks. Rhodes inspected the contents of his mug.

"Crook, what the hell is this?"

DC Steven Crook looked a little flustered. "What you asked for, gaffer: coffee, one sugar, a touch of milk."

"*A touch of milk*? It looks like you drowned a bloody cow in it."

"Mine's great – thank you, Crook," added DS Roberts.

"Yours would be – he fancies you. Watch out though, you don't know what he's stirred that with," mumbled Murray, his mouth half-full of sandwich.

Jackie Roberts glared at him before patting Crook on the back. "Don't worry, he's only jealous. Playboy over there thinks everyone should fancy him."

Rhodes, amused, watched his team with a kind of paternal pride. This was what it was all about. He knew that, though they sounded like a circus act now, in twenty minutes time they'd be sitting listening to DCI John Graham's briefing as professionally as ever. Meanwhile, they enjoyed each other's company.

"Gaffer, why you out here with us *mere mortals* anyway?" Murray asked.

"Just having a chat with *Master*."

"What have you been up to now?" Roberts asked Bates, sipping on her coffee.

"Fuck all," said DC Glenn Bates. Ten years as the target for office insults due to his unfortunate nickname had still not trained him to control his short temper.

"He wanted to show me a bit of info he got hold of. Seems he's got evidence of a gang of youths entering King of Chicken about five minutes after the railway attack."

"I know that place, it's not bad," Murray said, licking brown sauce from his index finger.

"I always try to avoid food served by an establishment with initials that spell out KOC," said Roberts, switching on her computer.

"What was I saying just the other day, Crook? She's not interested in men – she's just openly admitted she avoids cock!" Murray said without looking up from his monitor.

"Very funny, *Playboy*, maybe that's the reason I've been avoiding you, because you're the biggest *cock* in the room!" Even with her back to the others she knew Murray was about to speak. "Before you say it I said you *are*, not you have."

The young sergeant didn't acknowledge Roberts; more interested now in what the DI had said.

"So it's possible Stone is telling the truth?"

"You should know by now that in our line of work anything is possible. It still doesn't explain the lack of injury."

"That's easily explained," Roberts piped up.

"Oh really, *Sherlock*? Enlighten us!"

Roberts span in her chair, scooping up a green cardboard file filled with papers.

"He was drunk and he's a man, and men have a tendency to exaggerate things when they have a couple of beers. You of all people should know that, Playboy." She swaggered out of the office and into a meeting room on the opposite side of the corridor.

"She's got a point, Playboy," Crooks added.

Rhodes shook his head at the sound of his office phone ringing out just behind him. "See you all in fifteen minutes, Room 20, for the DCI's breifing. He's not happy: press are all over this."

Rhodes answered his phone. It was DCI John Graham.

45

"One second Sir." Rhodes walked to his door and went to shut it, calling, "Hey, Crook! That tasted liked a milky shit."

His door closed.

"How does he know what milky shit tastes like?" Crook asked, throwing the question out to the now bustling office.

NINE

DCI Graham's briefing was short and about as sweet as a pint of thick creamy bitter. To say he was not happy was an understatement. Annoyed by the slowness of any developments, he was of the opinion that *someone* must have seen *something*, which was an encouragement to Rhodes, who was happy they were both heading in the same direction for once.

Graham passed all authority for the Flynn case over to the new senior investigating officer, Patrick Rhodes. The DCI explained he was struggling with an ever-increasing list of policing issues, mainly down new government guidelines on cutbacks and overtime. This was a strange appointment: Graham had wanted to be part of every investigation since he'd taken over two months ago. This was the biggest case he'd had since he'd first taken the role, but Rhodes got the distinct impression the DCI wanted to be well out of it. Not that it bothered him in the slightest; besides, he was more experienced than Graham anyway.

*

Rhodes was sitting in his office, his face buried in a mountain of paperwork, files littered ever available inch of the carpet. There was a pile for closed cases that needed to be filed; there was a much bigger pile of unsolved cold case files. Outside his office the CID room buzzed, phones rang, officers entered and exited the room, busily working on their daily tasks.

DS Roberts was one side of the office talking to her team of DCs working on a drugs case; Murray was sitting at his station deep in a telephone conversation. Apart from the small lead of that gang at King of Chicken, which DC Crooks was now in the field following up, everything else on the Flynn case was as it had been for two days.

Things were so slow that DC Jake Bullen had been sent to a haulage company just south of Kidderminster, taking statements after a report had come in about employees receiving serious death threats.

Rhodes took out his personal phone and dialed Sadie; it didn't ring for long before switching to voicemail.

"Hi, it's Sadie, I can't answer your call right now. I'm really busy," there was loud laugh, which made Patrick smile before his daughter carried on, "seriously I am. If this is Dad I'm in a lecture and not a student bar, if it's anyone else I'm definitely in a bar. Anyway, leave a message and I'll call you back,"

Rhodes paused. Finally, he cleared his throat. "Hi, love. It's Dad. Just ringing to see if you're okay, haven't had chance to speak in a while. Mom says you're doing fine. The new house is nice, not home though and really quiet without you. Anyway, hopefully catch up with you later, love you, bye."

He disconnected and popped his phone back into his pocket.

Three Bullets

His mind wandered as he glanced at the clock on the wall. Please be in a class and not a bar, Sadie – it's only 11am.

TEN

Thursday was possibly the worst morning of the week so far for Daniel Stone, which was no mean feat considering how the week had begun.

Monday he'd been made redundant before nine in the morning.

Tuesday he woke up in a hospital to be interrogated by, in his opinion, a slightly deranged policeman.

Wednesday he spent most of the day talking to an elderly patient in the next bed about the underlying effects of kidney stones on the urinary tract.

Today had started okay; he'd managed to get dressed – a pretty major positive, he considered. He was sitting at a desk in the office of Kidderminster job centre when his day plummeted off a cliff. For over twenty minutes he'd listened to the scripted ramblings of a man who looked like he'd just left school, advising Daniel on how best to get a job.

Jason – which was what the man's name-tag said, although, an idiot like the one sat in front of Daniel now could very easily have put the *wrong* name-tag on – was jabbering on about some form that needed to be filled out.

Daniel had actually stopped listening a while ago; his eyes were focused on a dark chewing gum stain shaped like a lopsided crown on the dark blue carpet. His hand twisted the cap on the bottle of pain-killers in his pocket so it clicked every time he did one complete lap of the stain outline with his eyes.

This was the last thing he needed – some jumped-up spotty-faced little urchin lording it over him because he didn't have a job.

"In my experience…"

Daniel knew he was becoming angry because the clicks from the cap quickened. The clicks were now so close that he decided he simply couldn't hear any more words.

He stood up and heard Jason shouting across the office as he strode away. *In his experience!* What experience? He was still having his nappies changed when Stone had received his first payslip.

Daniel could hear his name being called out more frequently and in a higher pitch now; he didn't turn, just stuck out his elbows, using them as battering rams to push past a horde of brand-name-wearing youngsters. They looked like the runners-up of the sperm race: the sort of lazy, disfigured, weak specimens that wandered about in all directions with the deluded outlook that what they were doing was eventually going to amount to some sort of achievement. Daniel slammed out of the door and headed down the road.

ELEVEN

For someone who rarely drank, Daniel was becoming fairly accomplished in the art. Three-thirty in the afternoon and the only thing stopping him from lying face down on his gravel drive was the support from the PVC architrave of his front door.

Daniel juggled a hot kebab from hand to hand, the morning's fresh hand-dressing already stained with chilli sauce. Attempt number five was about to commence, the house key held shaking an inch from the hole.

Daniel stabbed it forward, his best shot so far, still inches wide of the target. Falling backwards, a slither of chicken kebab escaped from its garlic mayo pitta prison.

"Shit me! Why did you do that?" he asked, squinting his eyes to focus on the meat that he was now swinging uncoordinated arms toward. Like an out of time pendulum of a grandfather clock, he missed the food again.

Finally, more out of luck than skill, his fingers clung to the greasy prisoner and he shoved it deep it into his mouth.

"Got you!" he mouthed, spitting out grit and dirt.

An elderly lady, dragging her yapping Yorkshire terrier past, gave Daniel a look of utter disgust. She nearly walked straight into a middle-aged white-haired man dressed in a charcoal grey suit, who stood at the end of Daniel's drive.

"You okay? Need some help?" the man said.

Daniel jumped up, steadying himself on the boot of his Vauxhall.

"I'm good, thanks. I've got everything under control," Daniel assured him, trying hard to focus.

"Looks like it."

The man stepped forward just in time to catch Daniel as his stumble turned in to a complete loss of balance.

"Hey, you're the guy from the train," said Daniel.

The man walked Daniel to his front door and prised the key from his fingers.

"You know, I'm sure I needed you for something but I can't put my finger on it." The door opened and Daniel staggered in. "Come in! I've got a few bottles in the fridge."

"Just going to see you're okay, then I'll fuck off."

*

Jakub Tesar stood in the entrance hall of the house; it was cool, a lot cooler than the stifling heat outside. He wiped his brow with a handkerchief and released his feet from his slip-on leather shoes, leaving them close to the door. He removed his phone from his pocket and switched it off; he made sure the power had completely gone before entering the even cooler kitchen ahead. The grey tiled floor was heaven against his feet; he left a thin steaming footprint against the surface, which stayed for a few seconds before it evaporated.

"Funny seeing you again. Small world, isn't it?" said Daniel.

He handed Jakub a bottle of lager and took a sip from his own.

"Cheers. Not really that small."

A blank expression covered Daniel's face; he watched as Jakub placed his briefcase on the granite work-surface, clicking it open.

"I've been looking for you. In truth I have been *following* you. I saw you coming out of the doctor's and I've been on your tail ever since." Jakub grinned, "You have a really fucking boring existence, and that pub you were in, well, shithole doesn't begin to describe it."

"The doctor's? That was over, that was over…"

"Three hours ago."

Daniel stopped spooning ice cream from a tub into a bowl. His head was filled with meaningless, alcohol-induced thoughts, like, what would ice cream taste like if I poured my lager on it?

It normally took Daniel a lot longer to sober up than he was now.

He looked up at Jakub and stepped back. He tried hard not to show any fear. An image pushed past the jumbled contents of his head; his hands trembled against the dark wood. It was him!

"I got my story wrong, didn't I? It was you, you attacked that girl. I came up the ramp and you were attacking that girl, I tried to stop you and that's when you turned on me. Come back to finish the job, have you?"

"What kind of wanker do you think I am? I didn't attack any fucking girl." Jakub's hand moved deep into the briefcase that was turned so its contents were only visible to him.

"But you were there – I remember!"

"Where the fuck was I?"

Daniel moved in slow motion. His fingers felt for the handle on the door. "On the station, the night I got attacked. Tell me it was you that scared those arseholes off."

"Yeah, that was me; just call me fucking Superman. You owe me one. Well, two – I'm here to help you. I listened to your story on the train and how your life was spiralling into a shithole and I felt sorry for you. I want to help you out a little."

"You're here to help me?" Daniel tried to stall. He didn't believe Jakub for a second. Something in Jakub's voice scared him, and now his head was filled with escape plans that disappeared into emptiness every time he tried to pin one down.

"Yes, I am."

Daniel's knuckles began to lose colour; the tightness of his grip on the door handle turned them a whitey-grey. He began to push the handle down, aware that Jakub was not paying attention.

"I told the police that you were there; they said you weren't. You need to come forward – get me off the hook."

"You told the fucking filth? Listen, they're playing you, hoping you crumble and admit to something you didn't do – just so they can close the case."

Jakub's eyes dug into Daniel.

"You need to tell them what happened; you need to back me up, otherwise I could go to prison," said Daniel.

"I would get your arse prepared, pretty boy, because I won't be telling them fuckers anything. How much did you tell them? Did you mention the gun?"

"I had to tell them everything, everything I could remember anyway. For God's sake, Jakub! I didn't know what was going on; they thought I'd attacked that girl!"

Jakub's hand flashed from the case and he pointed a black semi-automatic pistol at Daniel, his finger on the trigger.

"So you told them I was carrying this?"

Jakub cracked the briefcase shut and took a long slow pull on his lager.

"Go and get comfy in the living room," he motioned with the gun toward the front room, "then we can talk about my offer, which might just get you out of the shit."

TWELVE

There was no clock of any description in his living room; even the DVD and Blu-Ray players didn't show the time. It wasn't something Daniel had ever noticed before; he had never really needed to look for one. He had a watch, and if for some reason he wasn't wearing it, his Sky remote would bring up the time. Daniel could only guess how long he'd been sitting on the brown studded leather sofa, playing over in his head what might happen now.

Though he could have sworn only minutes had passed, the four empty beer bottles beside Jakub hinted at a longer period.

Jakub was grinning to himself, taking slow pulls on his fifth bottle.

Daniel twisted his arm a fraction to get a glimpse of his watch, but the sunlight reflected onto the glass face, making it unreadable.

People were supposed to find solace in their own homes; Daniel would have traded any emotion for the outright terror that engulfed his body now. The chemical imbalance was overwhelming, causing fierce stomach cramps; his forehead muscles – in constant use fighting hard to keep his drooping eyelids from closing – hurt like hell.

The room was silent save for Jakub's fingers drumming against the gun, which was resting on the arm of the chair and pointing straight at Daniel.

"That offer, shall we go through the details again?"

Daniel looked up, his eyes half shut, the whites pink and dry.

"Before you fall a-fucking-sleep again." Jakub threw his empty bottle on the floor with the others, "You listening?"

Daniel went to speak, but the dryness of his throat stopped him. He nodded.

"Good. I'm going to offer you a way out of all the shit you're in, and all you need to do is give me three names." Jakub explained, his finger touching the trigger of the gun, waiting for a reply.

No reply materialised.

Jakub smiled, his perfect white teeth glinting in the sun, even whiter-looking now against the lager-induced red flush of his face.

"Three names for three free bullets. You know the difference between free bullets and normal bullets don't you?"

Daniel shook his head.

"A free bullet has no consequence." He waited for a response, none came. "You hear me? No fucking consequence, no capture, no evidence left, you can kill whoever you want and you'll get away with it."

Jakub was now standing in the centre of the room, waving the gun, pretending to fire at his own reflection in the mirror.

"Bang, bang, bang!" Each bang was accompanied by a wrist jerk and a dark smile into the glass. "That's how easy it is – three fucking bullets for three names; you could kill any son of a bitch you like! I'll even pull the trigger for you if you like, because I can see you're a pussy. Come on, it's an offer every goddamn person on this planet would love to get. To be able to kill not one, not two, but three of the people they hate the most.

"I'm not interested."

"Your interests have no relevance. It's going to happen, so come on, someone's got to have pissed you off enough for you to want them dead, even if for just a fleeting moment. Just give me one name."

"Harry."

"Who's Harry?"

Daniel had gotten Jakub's attention.

"He's a wizard," replied Daniel with a smile.

For a man in his late fifties and carrying as much weight as he was, Jakub moved fast and was now above Daniel on the sofa. The barrel of the gun was forced against Daniel's temple; Jakub's face was purple with rage.

"You think I'm fucking joking? I'm here to offer you a way out and you want to fuck with me? You have no idea what I'm capable of. I could show you some magic and make the back of your head appear on that wall!"

The force of Jakub's body pushed his victim against the cold leather sofa.

"Tell you what, give me two names and I'll give you some time to think about the other. You were a salesman, you should know how it works: you give a little, I give back, we bullshit for a while, then we meet in the middle with a result that benefits us both. Two names, go on, who were the last two people to piss you off?"

There was still no reply from Daniel.

Jakub released the pressure of the gun.

"I'll give you another chance. I'm in a pretty good mood you see – shagged some dirty dog last night, and you'll never guess what she let me do to her. Go on, guess."

"No idea."

"Well, let me just say she liked it, a lot."

Jakub took a pen from his inside pocket and placed it in Daniel's hand. He then took an envelope from his inside pocket.

"Scribble the names on there."

"This is addressed to me."

It may have been the knee pressing deep into his ribs that squeezed the words from the pen. He looked down at the scribble, four words that sent his hands into a spasm that he couldn't control.

Jakub sat back down in the armchair. He read the note, having placed the gun back on the armrest.

"See, that was easy. Very interesting. From our conversation on the train I understand the first one, but even I didn't see the second one coming."

Jakub rose from the chair and approached Daniel, who quivered on the sofa. He gave him a rough squeeze, took the pen from his hand and slipped it into the inside pocket of his suit jacket.

Daniel couldn't speak. He felt pain in his tear ducts but held back the tears.

Through his fat fingers Daniel could see untidy writing on the scrunched-up paper. Jakub prised Daniel's lips apart and forced the paper into his mouth.

"Swallow it!"

It was pointless to object; Daniel suspected Jakub would make him swallow it in the end – may as well get it over with. He began to chew, then he felt Jakub's fingers grip the sodden paper and wrench it back from his mouth.

"Changed my mind; I may need this," Jakub said as he brushed the excess saliva from the note and placed it in his suit pocket with the pen.

"You don't mind if I sleep the night, do you? You do have a spare room?"

Daniel gave a nervous nod, his head spinning.

"I'm going to crash out if that's ok – those beers have really hit me hard. Got some work to do in a couple hours. Sleep well if I don't see you later!"

"No, you're not stopping here; you need to go before I call the police."

Daniel watched from under his increasingly heavy eyelids as this man who'd spent the best part of the day terrorising him walked calmly across the living room, picked up the gun and turned back toward him.

Jakub climbed the stairs, before his head poked between the spindles of the bannister.

"I'm not fucking with you."

Daniel waited for Jakub Tesar to disappear upstairs before he ran to the kitchen. There it was a tiny piece of paper resting on the work-surface.

We will speak in the morning
Tell anyone I'm here and bullet No. 3 will be snugly lodged in your fucking head.

Overcome by emotion, Daniel collapsed in a heap on the floor.

What was going on? It felt like some twisted hidden-camera show, however, so far no one had jumped from behind a garden fence and said, 'Gotcha!'

Daniel peered upstairs; it was quiet.

He took out his mobile phone, returned to the kitchen, closed the door and began to dial a number. His finger hovered over the number nine for a few seconds, then he pressed it three times.

It rang and a lady answered: "What emergency service do you require?"

He paused. She repeated herself. Then Daniel heard the floorboards above him creak.

"I'm sorry, my son just got hold of my phone, really sorry for wasting your time."

"No problem sir, are you sure there is not an emergency?"

"No, just an accidental push of a button, really sorry."

Daniel disconnected the call and began to cry.

THIRTEEN

A maroon Vauxhall Vectra indicated off the A451 ring-road, turned onto the one way system and followed the road past Morrisons and Aldi before coming to at standstill at the traffic lights.

Alex Burns turned the volume down on the two-way radio and watched a group of teenage girls waiting impatiently at the front of a building.

Dixon Street had been home to two nightclubs for as long as Alex could remember, changing names every few years or so as publicity stunt. Names such as Redwoods, DY10, and Mirage had adorned the old brick work in striking fonts. There were posters plastered across the buildings which enticed the revellers inside to night spots that usually failed to deliver the excitement the posters outside projected.

Some young, flash businessman had taken over the one that used to be named Home – the one that had the queue outside now – and with a subtle nod toward the town's history named it The Carpet Rooms. Slick, flowing gold lettering on the bricks were an attempt to attract a more upper-class clientele.

Alex pulled away from the lights and passed the club, taking in some of the flesh on show. From the clothes that some of the girls nearly had on, he guessed that Thursday night's clientele was far from upper class. In fact, class was something they definitely lacked.

Alex turned right at the next set of lights into New Street. A green Nova raced toward him head on from Castle Street, causing Alex to slam on the brakes.

"Arsehole!"

He slammed down on the accelerator, the car sped off in pursuit of the Nova, which disappeared around the back of the college and came to a halt in the vast Tesco supermarket car park.

Alex parked his taxi a row away. He couldn't tell who was driving as the windows were blacked-out. He rushed to his boot. Hidden inside a large black Adidas gym bag was a crow-bar. Not standard taxi-driver issue, but weapons were becoming as essential as a sat-nav of late; there just in case some drunk tried to do a runner. Alex's weapon of choice was the crow-bar; others used pepper spray, some even carried knives or metal bars under their passenger seats. He took hold of the crow-bar now and slammed the boot down.

Four young lads got out of the Nova and pointed at Alex, laughing as they made their way across the car park.

Suddenly, Alex noticed a police car parked three spaces away. He slowly re-opened the boot, placed the tool under the bag, shut it with a bang and made his way into the store.

Green Street was a quiet place to hide.

A fog of fumes spat out into the darkening night sky from the rusting exhaust pipe. Alex rested his head half out of the open driver's side window, listening to the jobs being called out on the radio, his thoughts as incomplete as the clouds above.

An empty energy drink can lay next to two half-open packs of paracetemol, a Mars bar wrapper and a *Men's Health* magazine. The sweet citrusy smell of the energy drink clashed with the lavender air fresher, producing a noxious environment.

"Got a pick-up from College Walk over to Blockbuster Video and back," came a gruff female voice over the radio.

"Got that, Julie," a man replied.

There was silence again and Alex closed his eyes. Just a few minutes sleep – that would be okay.

"Any drivers want a Kidderminster Hospital to Worcester A&E, name of Stimson? Be warned, though, might be blood to clean up."

His finger flinched on the button of his control to call it in for himself; he hesitated and another driver took it.

"Alex?" Julie called out.

"Yeah?"

"Oh, so you are working tonight. I have a fare from outside Tesco Express on Comberton Hill. She wants taking into Worcester – asked for you by name."

"Sorry, can't do it. I'm feeling really ill – might clock off for the night,"

"Not an option, love, already three drivers down. I'll tell her five minutes, yeah?"

Even with his lack of enthusiasm for the job, it didn't take five minutes to drive the short journey to the Tesco. Alex indicated and pulled in to a parking space alongside the road. He looked out for someone who looked like they were waiting.

The car door opened. Tammy Cavendish leaned into the car and smiled; Alex closed his eyes in despair.

"Hi," she purred, climbing into the passenger seat, her tiny denim skirt riding up her legs so the tops of her thighs were visible. Alex saw this and fixed his eyes on it for a second or two.

"Where to?"

"Worcester."

"It's a big place – anywhere specific, or you just want me to drop you by the Elgar statue and you figure it out from there?"

"Riverside."

Alex knew Riverside, a fashionable club; a much more experienced clubbers' establishment than anything Kidderminster had to offer.

He pulled away.

Tammy leaned forward and turned the radio up; music rattled the door speakers.

Alex snapped the volume back down.

"Don't!"

"Just wanted to get in the mood."

The Worcester road was a long dual-carriageway and seemed to be taking much longer than usual; Alex fixed his eyes on the red lights of the line of cars in front. He managed to offer a few one-word answers to Tammy's constant interrogation, most of which focused on his personal life.

They entered Worcester City and headed toward the racecourse, turning at a set of lights, passing Worcester Police Station and then the American diner Detroit's. Alex stopped his car.

"Eighteen pound."

"You okay to pick me up later? I'll come back to yours then."

Tammy flashed a bit more leg. Her hand moved across and rubbed up along Alex's leg.

He pushed it away.

"Working till four."

"I'll be out about two. Shall I call you?"

"I'll be on a job."

Alex struggled to control himself, it wasn't every day a young girl offered no strings sex. She was very attractive; a little fake but, underneath the thick caramel foundation and black eyeliner, she was pretty. Definitely someone Alex would try to get into bed if he was out drinking. Her slim, toned body turned Alex on, but something wasn't quite right and he questioned if having sex would be a clever thing to do, especially knowing who her father was.

"Wouldn't you like to see me safely tucked up in bed?"

"Call the rank later, see if I'm free."

Tammy leaned across and kissed Alex on the lips. She smelt so good, her moist lips pressed against his. She rubbed the crotch of his jeans and squeezed his penis; he was hard, which she seemed to relish.

"I think you'll be free," she said and leaned closer to Alex. "You ever raped a girl, Alex?" she whispered.

Alex reeled backward.

"Fucking get out!"

Tammy smiled.

"I'll take that as a maybe," she smiled. "Save the innocent face for the police. Don't turn up later and they'll be asking you exactly that question tomorrow morning."

"What is wrong with you?"

Tammy tugged a little at her light-pink vest top. "It's quite easy to rip a few pieces of clothing and cry wolf nowadays, especially with what happened to that Flynn girl at the station. The police would be over you like an STD."

"You wouldn't!"

She dropped a twenty pound note in his lap and tapped it. "See you later. Don't look so scared, sexy, be proud that I chose you."

From her peach-coloured clutch bag she pulled a pack of three condoms and squeezed them into Alex's pocket.

"I'll be back for them later – all of them."

Alex watched in horror as Tammy strutted down the cobbled pathway towards the club.

Did he dare risk not coming back?

The paracetamol seemed to stop working in an instant, and his brain felt like it was fighting its way out of his skull. He leaned across and turned off his radio.

Two cars behind Alex's, another taxi stood stationary, its engine running. The driver's face was hidden behind the shadow of the sun-visor, pulled down even though it was now dark. The driver was looking in the same direction, watching Tammy Cavendish.

FOURTEEN

Patrick Rhodes opened the pristine front door of his new house and stepped from the humid evening air into the cool magnolia hallway. An old German Shepherd plodded along the carpet to greet his master.

"Hiya, mate."

Rhodes patted the dog, remembering to be gentle; the years had started to catch up and anything more than a gentle pat would result in a feeble whimper. The dog raised his head before returning to the kitchen and slumping comfortably onto a worn blanket.

Rhodes threw his keys and warrant card down onto the telephone table near the door; he picked up a stack of letters neatly placed at an angle against the phone.

The first one read 'Mr. Rinshaw'.

"Who the hell is Mr. Rinshaw? Why can't people get things right? Look it's not even this house number, not even the goddamn same street, Scally!"

The dog tilted his head a fraction at the sound of his name, then closed his eyes.

Patrick entered the kitchen carrying the letters. Not one was addressed to him; he threw them down on the work-surface and picked up a note that was folded in a neat triangle.

This was one of the many things Rhodes loved about his wife. Her letter- and note-writing; even though she was more than capable of sending text messages she always left him a note. He began to read.

> *Your dinner's in the oven. Different house, same rituals – me cooking, you not here to eat. You don't like my cooking or something?*
> *Leaving Gemma's for airport at about 11. So call me if you can before 12. See you when I get back.*
> *There are some ready meals in the freezer for Scally; you know he doesn't like your cooking.*
> *Love you forever with all my heart.*
> *Rita*
> *XX*
> *X*

The writing was immaculate, all apart from a watermark in the middle of the words '*your cooking*', which looked like a teardrop had blotted the ink.

He took a deep breath. He hated it when she left. He knew he should have been on the plane with her. At first he had always blamed the job, but really it was the idea of getting on a giant metal seagull that frightened him. Seven years still remained on his third adult passport and not once had he actually stepped foot on foreign soil.

He felt guilty, empty.

She'd put up with a lot over the years, just got on with it. It couldn't have been easy being a policeman's wife: nights spent alone, the worry.

Patrick Rhodes loved his wife with all his heart and he would show her so, on her return. Once the Flynn case was over they'd book a holiday together. Abroad.

Rhodes read the note again, smiled and dialled his wife's phone.

"Hi love...sorry I missed you..."

He was interrupted by his work phone; it was the DCI.

"Sorry Rita, DCI's calling, I have to take this. Call you straight back."

Rhodes switched phones and activated the hands-free button, "Detective Inspector Rhodes," he said, taking the chicken dinner from the oven and placing it in the microwave. A loud hum started.

"Rhodes, we seem to have a development in the Flynn case."

"A development? What sort of development?"

"One of our friends over at the BTP was checking some CCTV and it's given us something else to work on; also, had an update from the hospital, which isn't great. I need you and your team in the briefing room for seven. We'll bring Roberts in on this one as well."

British Transport Police were involved, so it was either something they found on the train or some CCTV that his detectives had overlooked.

There was a pause as Rhodes lifted his plate from the microwave with a tea towel and took a taste of it. He spat the contents back onto the plate.

"I'll let them all know, Sir." Rhodes dropped his phone into his jacket pocket and slid the contents of the plate into Scally's bowl.

"Help yourself – you seem to like her cooking better than me!"

Rhodes swiped up his keys from the telephone table and stormed out, slamming the front door behind him.

Scally looked towards the door before tucking in to the food with a contented sigh.

FIFTEEN

Plastic is no match for solid oak, no matter how hard it has been made; Greg Flynn's mobile phone slipped from his grip, smashing into three separate pieces on the floor.

Greg forced his shoes on, not even taking the time do undo the laces. He checked the pockets of the suit jacket that hung on the back of the chair.

Sheila Flynn rushed from upstairs, her face grey with panic. "What is it, Greg?"

Greg found his keys and moved to the front door.

"Not good news."

"Oh God, no!"

"Just keep an eye on Max for me; if he wakes tell him I'll be back as soon as possible,"

The elderly lady just nodded, watching her son charge out of the door.

He pushed the button on his key-fob and the central-locking clicked with a flash of the headlights. He threw his jacket into the back and jumped into his six-day-old Jaguar XKR. The engine roared into life, a sound that thundered through the quiet street. His hand slammed his gearstick into reverse and with a gentle squeeze of his foot on the accelerator the car flew backwards. Greg saw in his rear view mirror that the gateway was blocked by a stranger. The rear lights lit up the stranger's legs.

"What are you doing?" Greg shouted, leaning out of the door.

The man didn't reply.

"Hey, dickhead! Did you hear me?"

Greg unclipped his seatbelt and jumped out of the car. The man stepped forward, a little unsteady on his feet, his face covered in part by a grey hooded jacket, the hood pulled low over his forehead, shadowing his eyes. He looked well-built, but the hoodie was baggy, so it wasn't clear how big he actually was.

"I'm sorry," the man mumbled.

"What was that?"

"I'm sorry."

Greg's patience was being seriously tested.

"Get the fuck off my drive!"

The hooded figure didn't move, and his eyes remained focused on the ground.

"I'm so sorry for what happened to your daughter."

Greg froze.

The light from the hallway washed across the gravel as Sheila opened the wooden, church-style front door.

"You okay, Greg? Who's that you're talking to?"

"Go back inside, Mother – make sure Max is okay. I'm sorting it."

Greg spun back around. "Do you want to tell me who the hell you are and why you're standing on my driveway? It's nearly midnight!"

The man moved towards Greg, who now prepared to defend himself.

"I'm just a guilty man, asking for forgiveness. I'm not sure what I've done, but it feels right to be here now."

Greg went to launch himself at the man; this had to be the man who had attacked his daughter. He just knew it. The light from the hallway once again broke his attention.

"Dad!" Max screamed.

The young boy stood there in his pyjamas, being held back by his grandmother.

"It's okay Max – I'm okay!"

He turned to speak to the man, but he was gone. Greg ran into the street but there was no sign of him in either direction. It was impossible for him to have disappeared, but he had – the man who'd just been standing on drive had vanished.

Greg phoned the police and explained, telling them he wanted someone there as soon as possible because he needed to be at the hospital. Returning to the house, he kissed Max on the head and told him he'd be back soon and to be good for his Nan; the police were on the way.

He got in his car and drove away, making sure to close the gates behind him.

As the Jaguar roared away, a man appeared from a neighbouring driveway; he strolled up to the gates and pushed his face against the cold iron, looking up at a window where light broke through a gap in the curtains.

FRIDAY: DAY 4

SIXTEEN

Through a sea of drunken revelers, thin blue laser lights jerked and span in time with the beat. A shrill female voice sang repetitive phrases over the thumping bass and a backing of synthesised keyboard sounds, which echoed around the walls.

To one side of this mass of sweat-drenched, gyrating bodies was Tammy, sitting on a sofa, looking towards the dancefloor, her back turned to a well-groomed, shaven haired-headed man sitting close to her. For the last half hour he had been paying more attention to Tammy's breasts than her face. His skintight white t-shirt shone violet under the neon lights.

Tammy felt the music vibrate from her toes upwards, seeming to concentrate around her chest; she felt as though the pressure might force its way out. She got a buzz from this feeling, greater than anything else, except sex.

This was Tammy's world: the deafening music, the sweet smell of sweat, the non-stop sexual arousal – this was where she belonged. Tonight it just didn't feel the same. There was something missing.

Her interest in the man by her side waned by the second; he talked too much, slurring into her ear. She could feel his spit on her neck.

Yes, he was interested in her chest – who wasn't?

Why hadn't he asked her back to his?

Why wasn't he pushing her against a wall this very second, pulling her pants to one side, doing exactly what she wanted? She didn't need a man who was going to take this long to get to the point.

Wrapping her lips around her straw, she drank till her glass was empty.

"Any chance of a drink?"

The lad gave a smile; picking up her glass, he leant in for a kiss. Tammy responded, but his breath was a vile, a mixture of cigarettes and lager.

The lad disappeared into the crowd around the bar.

She waited a few minutes and made her way to the exit.

A friend was waving and mouthing something. Tammy waved back and walked away. She gave one final smile to the bouncers before she swaggered down the street, her phone pressed against her ear.

"Hey sexy, I'm just leaving now. You're in for a great night – I've had some prick buying me Cheeky Vimtos all night. I'm a proper dirty bitch after a few of those. See you in a bit."

Tammy found a bench along a grassy area near the river and waited, tapping away on her phone, typing a Facebook status update.

A silver taxi pulled alongside and stopped, the driver's face hidden in the darkness. Tammy waved the taxi away; it didn't move. Putting her phone back to her ear, she peeked behind her. The taxi was still there.

"Alex, don't piss about, I really need you to pick me up - it's cold. I'll be over by the college car park."

She rose to her feet in a slow deliberate motion and stepped across the parched grass, which crunched like straw beneath her three-inch heels.

The car pulled away along the road. Tammy closed her eyes and a warm wave of relief washed over her. She made her way to the car park. Even in her drunken state her mind told her to stay close to the road, to stay in view of passing cars.

Turning a corner, Tammy raised a forced smile to a group of girls outside an Indian restaurant, and waited for a lorry to pass before crossing the road. She smirked as one of the girls tripped and slumped against a passing hunk – a trick Tammy had used many a time herself.

Then, to her horror, she spied the same taxi once more, sitting about fifty metres away. The headlights were switched off and the driver's door was ajar.

Tammy didn't wait to see who might emerge from the car, but turned and, quickening her pace, headed back to where she had come from, her fingers fumbling in her bag for her phone. A false nail snapped on the zip.

"Alex, some weirdo is following me." She glanced over her shoulder. "This isn't another one of my games. He got out a taxi and he's walking behind me."

Cold fear swept through her, stilling her heart, stopping her breath.

Tammy shuddered.

Another quick look – still there.

There was no-one she needed more right now than her father – most of the time she hated him, but now she just wanted him to step from anywhere and thrust his boulder fist into the face of the figure behind her.

Her heart jerked back into life, galloping in time with her step.

She stumbled. Her three-inch fake Louis Vuitton heels weren't great running attire. She slipped them off and held them as she ran.

Everything inside her was working too fast and she struggled to keep up with the pumping of her own lungs.

"I'm really scared, Alex. Forget what I said in your car, I didn't mean it. Please come get me, Alex! I'm so scared, oh God! Please come, Alex – please! Oh, fucking hell!"

It must have been splintered glass that caused pain to pulse through her foot – no time to stop and inspected it though. He was gaining; she could hear his footsteps getting closer. She winced every time her tender sole touched the pavement.

The coldness of his fingers on her soft skin tingled; they were firm and the force spun her round.

Tammy screamed, falling against a boarded-up shop window.

SEVENTEEN

The makeshift briefing room was quiet; of the six people sitting around the group of tables pushed together to make one large one, only DC Glenn Bates made any noise, his mouth full of gum. Bates was nursing the mother, father and seven or so other close relatives of a hangover; one drink watching the football with his brother in law had turned into a late night lock in. His exaggerated sighs and whimpers fell short of raising any questions from DS Jackie Roberts and DI Patrick Rhodes.

Rhodes was sipping coffee from a polystyrene cup and thumbing through a copy of *Worcestershire Life* magazine, sneaking peeks above it at DS Roberts. He admired her: her ambition, her ability to be one of the lads if needed and to then slip effortlessly into her role as one of the girls; most of all, her beauty.

He watched her drink from a can of Coke, her auburn hair in a tight bun, redder than ever against her pale complexion, her emerald eyes glinting through her fringe.

Schofield was baffled by her intake of Coke. He had told her once that they cleaned the lorry engines at the Coke factory with barrels of Coke. Her reply had been as quick and as clever as ever: she just smiled and said, well, they clean people's insides out by squirting what you're drinking up their arses – you still drink it!

Couldn't argue with that.

DS Roberts was the only woman he'd ever contemplated leaving his wife for.

PC Jonathan Curry sat closest to Rhodes, a young, pleasant, uniformed officer who'd been in charge of the scene at the railway station. He flicked through some notes in his pad. He'd been called in by Rhodes to give an update on the condition of Abbie Flynn, whose room he had spent ninety percent of his working time outside for the last four days.

Beside him was DC Tori Vilani; at twenty-nine, she was an experienced detective who worked with Rhodes on almost every case.

Mary Ann Watson sat looking a little out of place, a white-haired lady in her sixties, dressed in a bubbled grey cardigan and pale brown cotton trousers. Her face was covered in thick foundation. She was the scene of crime manager, a meticulous worker, widow of a retired policeman and an essential part of the team.

The door opened. Joel Murray gave a half-hearted salute and took a seat next to DC Bates.

"Drinking again last night was we, Master?" he asked.

"What makes you think that?"

"Just the stench of peppermint," he smiled.

"You ever thought about becoming a detective? I think you would be good at it," Bates replied, allowing himself a smirk. "How's the missus? Not long now, is it?"

"Two weeks; she finished work yesterday."

"She gone through that nesting period yet?" Rhodes asked.

"Nesting? You do know I'm married to a *woman* not a *duck*, right?"

"You need to take more notice, mate, nesting is when they —"

"Who are *they*?" Roberts snapped at Bates.

"Sorry, for the benefit of the females in the room, it's when the mother-to-be becomes maternal and wants to clean everything because she believes the baby's due."

"That'll explain why my shirts are all colour-coordinated all of a sudden, then."

A ripple of laughter broke out.

The door opened once more: Detective Chief Inspector John Graham strode in, placing a briefcase on the table and standing by the desk. DCI Graham was fairly new to the role of DCI; he had somehow managed to get the chief inspector's job even though he'd never worked a day of his career in CID. This hadn't gone down well in the office. No-one was more bemused by this decision than Rhodes, who, having spent six months as acting DCI, expected a permanent position.

The new inspector was disliked by everyone: he was arrogant, was not a team player and, in his short time in the job, seemed to lack direction, something the team had noticed and bitched about more than once. Within hours of his receiving the appointment, rumours that his race had played a part in his getting the job were flung about. And apparently, he'd never even wanted the position.

At thirty-eight, he was still athletic-looking and stylish: a balding Denzel Washington, say.

The team watched as Graham shuffled about, staring at the ground.

"Good morning. Thank you for coming in so early. It is 7.02am on Friday 20th April; this is the third briefing of

Operation Downbeat: the investigation into the assault of Miss Abbie Flynn at Kidderminster Railway Station."

DCI Graham went through a brief description of the details of the case from the notes he had prepared, then asked if anyone had any updates.

Glenn Bates raised his hand.

"Sir, I've been studying the CCTV from King of Chicken and have clear images of three of the five youths; I'll get them circulated this morning."

"Daniel Stone's search came back clean," said DC Vilani. "No DNA previously on record. The guy has one speeding fine for 36 in a 30; he paid his fine *and* went on a speed awareness course."

"Still waiting for result of the nail scrapings from both Stone and Flynn. The scene is now open to the public again, so anything we've missed is unlikely to be found now," Mary-Anne Watson said.

DCI Graham leaned over to his briefcase and pulled out The Sun, The Daily Mail and a print out from an online edition of The Shuttle, the local Kidderminster paper. "Any news on Stone's shoes?"

"No, Sir. I've got uniform to check homeless shelters and known night-spots; no-one has them unless they're just not showing them in public," said Rhodes.

"Keeping them for special occasions?" added Murray, which raised a few titters.

"Anything else before I add my developments?"

Silence.

"News from the hospital is bleak; parents were called last night to discuss switching off the life support," PC Curry announced. He looked at his notepad. "Going back down there after this meeting."

"Well, to be honest we should have been treating this as a murder case from the beginning. She was never going to survive," said Graham, slamming down the papers he was holding. "Here's the position I'm in. At present I have six detectives working this case. Now, on the evidence of what has been found so far I'd be better off firing each and every one of you and employing a bunch of hack reporters."

"Sir?" said Rhodes bemused.

"I must explain my utter embarrassment at this department."

Rhodes felt his blood boil. How could someone with so little experience in detective work walk into an office full of experienced officers and talk to them like they were just out of nappies.

"Do you know what the press are running with this morning? The victim is dying, and the police have no idea who is responsible. The press seem to believe that her *boyfriend* may have something to do with it. Did anyone in this office know she even *had* a boyfriend?"

"I asked, Sir, but her parents told me there was nothing serious," PC Curry answered, looking a little ashamed that he hadn't dug deeper.

"Her parents? For God's sake, she's nineteen! How many of your parents knew who you were screwing when you were nineteen?"

There were already foundations in place for a wall to be built between the CID and DCI Graham, and Graham seemed to be laying even more bricks with each new word he spoke.

"With all due respect, sir, you are talking about a dying girl," said Tori Vilani.

"With all due respect, Constable, I'm talking about a possible murder. The boyfriend, Toby Sinton. Our *friends* in the press have found him! Look, that's him smiling next to...oh who is that in the picture...correct me if you think I'm wrong...oh yeah, it's *Abbie Flynn*. According to the University of Lincoln, which again if anyone is interested is where Abbie Flynn studies, Toby, her boyfriend of *two years* has not been on campus for a week. Seems he's gone on a camping weekend with pals in the Forest of Dean. Glenn, Joel, hope you don't have any weekend plans, because you'll be tracking him down."

Graham played some CCTV. The others watched as the blurred screen showed Abbie Flynn standing near a taxi. The driver took a hold-all from the girl and put it in the boot before Abbie walked off camera. The driver got in, his back to the camera, and waited five minutes before driving off.

"The taxi is registered to Minster Cars, who operate out of an office in Blackwell Street. The taxi belongs to a Mr. Colin Templeton. He lives with his mother on Heron's Nest caravan park near Bewdley. Someone go and question him. See what he was doing at the station that night and why. After what looked like him giving Abbie a lift, did she then walk away from him? Jonathan, can you speak to Graham Flynn at the hospital, see if that hold-all has turned up?"

PC Curry nodded.

"Also, Mr. Flynn called last night regarding a trespasser on his drive. Jonathan, can you get the full details to me on that one? Anyone got anything else to add?"

No-one spoke.

DCI Graham thanked them for their time and asked to be kept informed, before leaving the room.

"Patrick, you need to get him out, before we have to investigate *his* murder," said Joel Murray.

DI Rhodes ignored the comment – he was already out the office following DCI Graham down the hall.

"Sir!"

DCI Graham stopped dead in his tracks and made a distinctly slow turn to greet Rhodes.

"Yes, *Inspector*?"

Rhodes caught the emphasis on the word 'inspector', but he wasn't going to rise to the bait.

"That room is full of good detectives. I think you need to start showing some respect!"

DCI Graham chewed his bottom lip.

"I don't need good detectives, Rhodes, I need this case solved. Forgive me if I don't give a shit about respect. Results are more important than respect, and you've been here long enough to know that. I need my figures to go in the right direction because that's all that matters in today's force. Maybe if results had been better before, you would be wearing my suit now."

"What would you know? You've never been a detective."

"No, you're right; and you've been a detective a long time, so do me a favour and start doing some detecting!"

Rhodes held his temper and merely smiled.

"You want my job, Rhodes, then mess this case up so they ship me out somewhere else."

"If I wanted your job, I would have had it by now."

"Good. Then find the attacker; it's making us all look bad."

DCI Graham walked away, leaving Rhodes alone in the corridor.

EIGHTEEN

Someone with OCD or maybe a person with a military background – they were the only people capable of making a bed with such precision and in complete silence. Standing in the spare room of his rented house, Daniel inspected the perfection in front of him. The lilac and white floral pattern of the quilt, crease free; the scatter cushions, stacked in an immaculate arrangement that made the bed look like a photo from some upmarket lifestyle magazine.

Daniel once again struggled with his memory; he knew he'd finished all the bottles in the fridge, although his unwanted guest had drunk five of the seven Buds. His mind should have been clear, but there was a groggy feeling: his throat was dry, his head and nose were congested.

After inspecting downstairs and the other bedroom Daniel was pretty sure his house was empty. The evening's Bud bottles stacked neatly along the kitchen window ledge told him that Jakub had already risen, tidied up after himself and gone.

It didn't add up: had he really just been joking? Did the job offer exist? Daniel toyed with the idea of calling the police, twice picking up the phone before replacing the handset before anyone answered.

Back upstairs, and feeling a little better, he decided to freshen up; he placed a pair of jeans and a navy t-shirt on his bed, wrapped a towel around himself and climbed in the shower.

The warm water felt good against his face. He opened his mouth and let the water roll down his face and spill over his chin. He felt alive for the first time all week. Daniel grabbed the thick cream towel from the radiator and walked to the bedroom, wrapping it around his waist. He looked himself up and down in the full length mirror, like he had every day since being discharged.

He was different today. Puffing out his chest and looking at his disappearing six pack, he made a mental plan to get this weekend out of the way then sort himself out. A new job, a gym membership, a new relationship – he wanted his life back.

He scratched at his unshaven face and smiled; he didn't care that Jakub had been there or, particularly, for his so called 'job offer'. Who would want to work for a man whose job offers were presented at gunpoint? He shuddered. If that was the offer, he dreaded to think what the team-building exercises would entail.

The week had passed quickly, and he was happy it was Friday. Daniel loved Fridays.

Friday, the day he was no longer alone in his life. The marital break-up had hit him hard; he spent his whole life trying his best to be a family man.

His son Ollie was his entire world, but it was a world that no longer existed as it once had. He lived now in a world he'd stumbled unconsciously into; just another weekend dad: cinemas, swimming baths, McDonalds – all the clichés.

Daniel returned to the bathroom, which now smelt of Deep Sea Mint mineral shower gel, and twisted the hot tap on. He took a razor from the cabinet and smeared shaving foam all over his face, still beaming at the thought of his son happily awaiting him at the school gates.

A three-day growth covered his tired face, and the bluntness of the blade left his skin red and sore. With one final rinse he caught sight of the cabinet mirror, which had steamed up from the heat of the running tap. There was a discordant clang as Daniel's razor fell into the sink. His enthusiasm for the day crumbled. He steadied himself against the bath.

In the steam on the mirror drawn with a finger was an uneven circular face with tears dripping from one eye, beneath were scrawled the words, 'BULLET 1 TODAY'.

NINETEEN

The town's police station was an ominous-looking, flat-fronted three-storey block. Like a medieval castle, it stood with vantage points on all four sides; an architectural statement all of its own, it seemed to say: 'we are the law; you don't want to mess with us!'

Standing at the point where three roads met, the station was set back from the road and housed an expansive car park and lawn. The main entrance ran through a two-storey, glass-fronted reception, refurbished five years before to give a sense of space, light and welcome.

Not that many of the station's visitors arrived with such sentiments in mind.

The reception's interior was sharp-lined, modern. The light from the windows spread through the space, lending it a sterile atmosphere. Three toughened-glass counters stood directly in front of the entrance, arranged in a curve which covered the back wall. Each counter stood at a different height, with the far right window at wheelchair level.

A Perspex sign showing the force's emblem hung on the far wall. Three locked security doors led off from the reception; one to the right and two to the left. The walls were plastered in posters. One read 'Domestic violence: don't keep it behind closed doors', and underneath a helpline number was printed. A second poster showed a hand slipping into a bag and said, 'Be aware, zip it up'.

Behind one of the windows sat a uniformed officer, her hair tightly curled into a bun held in place by what looked like a fishbone, her spectacles precariously perched on the end of her nose.

A youth dressed in white Adidas shorts, a vest and large trainers dropped his insurance documents into the security well. She thanked him, her words muffled behind the toughened glass.

The first of the four chairs was occupied by a grinning Colin Templeton, his yellow, infected toenails poked from a pair of dirty grey flip-flops. A pair of three-quarter length cargo trousers revealed his pasty, skeletal legs. His outfit was finished with a stained white t-shirt.

When the lad finished giving the receptionist a mouthful about being victimised because his car was, in his words, "A fucking pussy magnet, and the pigs were just jealous," Colin walked to the desk.

"You get me, innit," the lad said to Colin as he folded his paperwork in his pocket.

"Oh yeah, I got you *big time*, brother," Colin replied, showing a grin that covered the whole of the lower part of his face.

"Don't spit me any shit, Grandad," shouted the lad as he slammed the entrance door behind him.

"I'm sure that's the last thing I would like to be spitting."

The officer stared now at Colin over the rim of her glasses.

"Can I help you?"

Colin looked at her, jabbed his finger up his nose, rummaged around for a few seconds, inspected the contents of his nail before wiping it on the counter.

"I think it's more how I can help you. I hear information regarding the Abbie Flynn attack is in short supply. Luckily, I've got some."

The officer stopped scribbling on her pad. Her first impression was that this guy was just another weirdo looking to get some information, a bit of personal pleasure. The town was full of coffin-chasers, most of them carrying clip-boards and hoping to gain some injury insurance claim out of the victim. She looked deep into his eyes, which sent a cold trickle down her back.

"Could I take some details? Then I will pass your information on to the correct department; they will contact you if we need any further information."

Colin felt a ball of anger building in his stomach.

"I'm sorry – did you not hear me? I have info."

"Sir, I heard you clearly, and if I can take some details…"

The bang of Colin's hand on the counter echoed around the high ceiling and wooden walls of the corridor.

"If I was to come in here and tell you I attacked her, would you just take some details and contact me if you needed any more info?"

"Did you attack Abbie Flynn, sir?"

"No – of course not!"

"Well, in that case, sir, if I could just take some details…"

"No. No, I don't think you understand – if I don't speak to DI Rhodes, people could die." He shrugged his shoulders and twitched his eyes toward the door. "Who knows, there might be someone else dying right this second."

The receptionist struggled to keep her composure and flicked through some papers, trying not to take too much notice of Colin's anger. Behind her in the office a young girl stood at a photo-copier working, too far away to hear what was being said, she just looked over and smiled.

"I don't think he's in, sir."

"I watched his Audi pull into the staff car park three hours ago, and unless his car has moved in the last ten minutes, then he's in."

The officer traced her finger down a list and dialled Rhodes's extension.

"Hi, it's Ange. Yes, thank you, are you? I have someone who really needs to speak to you, says he has info on the Flynn case… No, he said he'll only talk to you." She listened for a minute. There was a short pause before she put the phone down.

"Take a seat – he's on his way down."

"Thank you. If only all women were as well-behaved as you, the world would be a much safer place," said Colin before he returned to the seat he'd been sitting in earlier.

TWENTY

Jackie Roberts didn't slow down, flying toward the green and yellow John Deere, before pulling into a small cut-in at the last second. The tractor's driver gave a wave and smile through the mud smeared window; Roberts obliged with a wave of her own.

She pulled out again, and the needle of the speedometer jerked to attention.

The hedgerows were high; trees hung down, blocking out the sky and creating the impression of a tunnel, and that they were going much faster than they actually were. A pheasant darted from the hedge. Crooks let out a minute squeal; Roberts looked at her colleague cowering, smiled, then touched the brakes. The bird disappeared back into the greenery.

"You trying to get us killed?"

"Relax, I know these lanes."

She did.

In fact, this was the very lane where her granddad had taught her to drive in his Austin Allegro, and they were heading to the very same caravan park where she'd spent most of her school holidays in her grandparents' sardine tin of a caravan. The plywood box covered with corrugated metal sheet and a leaky, flat tin-roof looked nothing like the ones that now came in view. She pulled past the park sign and a six foot wooden heron and into the car park.

"Wow, wasn't expecting that," Crooks remarked.

"My driving, or how nice some of these are?" said Roberts, looking at a row of sparkling mobile homes.

"Both."

They crossed the car park to an L-shaped wooden lodge with 'Reception' printed on the door.

In front of them stood an impressive lodge with a green-tiled, pitched roof and double-glazed patio doors, surrounded by acacia. A luxurious brown leather sofa was visible through the window; the lodge itself was surrounded by white PVC decking.

"That one's bigger than my flat," DC Crooks announced as they entered the office.

The office was like the inside of a Swedish sauna, with walls and ceiling clad in jatoba wood. Eight large spotlights lit up the room; brochures and leaflets lay fanned on a table.

Beyond a large counter sat Angela and Samantha Wilde, both deep in telephone conversation. The younger of the two held up a finger to indicate that she'd registered the two detectives; she was in her early twenties, slim, fair-haired and with a slightly crooked smile. As soon as she'd finished her call she made her way to the counter.

Crooks was engrossed in a 2013 Willerby model guide.

"Good morning, can I help?"

Roberts introduced herself and her colleague, and asked if they could get directions to the home of Colin Templeton. The girl took out a site map and pointed to the plot that Mrs. Templeton's home was on.

"Mom, going to show these officers to a plot."

The other lady, who looked nowhere near old enough to be the girl's mother, nodded.

The detectives followed Samantha out of the office, around the security barrier and past a row of modern caravans.

Crooks was amazed at how chirpy the young girl was, twice stopping to talk to residents who were resting on benches in their immaculate gardens, and giving a running commentary on the park as she went.

"How much would one of this set me back?" Crooks asked.

"Depends. We can go through a few details after, if you like."

Roberts grinned; she felt like she was witnessing the birth of an innocent teenage romance – though both parties were about a decade late.

"I might pop back tomorrow if that's okay, that's if you're here tomorrow. Never knew places like this existed. Well, I knew they were about, just thought they were more like that gypsy wedding programme."

Roberts and the girl chuckled at Crooks, who was becoming increasingly flustered.

Samantha stopped and pointed to a small older caravan. It was different to the others; the plot was unkempt and the caravan was grimy. She told the detectives that her mother was forever trying to speak to Mrs. Templeton and her son about tidying the place up, or they would be forced to move off. They never took any notice.

Roberts climbed the two large steps leading to the door and knocked. She called Colin Templeton's name and announced who she was. There was no answer; she knocked again and again, but there was no reply.

"She's in, never goes out!" Sam called back to them from the path.

DC Crooks tried the handle; it was unlocked and the door opened. He leapt backwards, his eyes bulging, and spat on the floor, gagging and coughing.

"What the hell is that smell?" Roberts asked, covering her nose and mouth.

"Smells like sewerage," Samantha answered.

"More like dog shit!" Crooks added, as he poked his head into the van.

He covered his mouth and stepped inside; there was no one in the living area. It was clean and warm. Photos and ornaments decorated the maple cupboards above the fireplace. He continued through the spotless kitchen area and along the narrow hallway. The smell intensified; he used the end of his torch to push open a door that was slightly ajar.

He retched at the sight of Mrs. Templeton, her drab nightdress riding up over her rippled stomach as she lay slumped over a double bed, her covers drenched in tar-like faeces and her carpet sodden with bright yellow urine. A colostomy bag hung from the mattress, overflowing with thick human waste.

His eyes were drawn now to her face: her skin as dark as rainclouds, her lips like a winter sky. Crooks crept over, avoiding the lumps of waste, and pressed two fingers to her neck – no pulse, and she was cold.

Roberts tapped the door and Crooks jumped.

"Shit me, Jackie: if it's not your driving, it's your sneaking about that's going kill me."

"I'll call this in," came her unfazed reply.

Crooks lowered Mrs. Templeton's eyelids and went back outside; Roberts had notified for an ambulance and was now calling the coroner. Crooks took long deep breaths, filling his lungs with fresh country air.

"She's dead?" asked Samantha, on overhearing the female detective's phone conversation.

"Yep, and by the looks of it she's been that way a good eight, nine hours," Crooks replied, wiping spit from his chin.

"No, that can't be right!" Samantha started to look anxious.

"I'm afraid she is."

"No, you don't understand - her son only left the park about three hours ago."

TWENTY-ONE

The interior of Detective Inspector Rhodes's office was starting to look more like that of a hide in a nature reserve. There were half a dozen gold-framed photos of birds on the left wall, equally spaced to form a circle. Two of the photos showed rare birds he'd spotted whilst in his late teens, before the force had taken over all of his free time – one a Little Whimbrel he had seen in 1984, and the other a Red-breasted Nuthatch, the only one ever seen in Britain, in 1989. Both these birds were seen in Norfolk, a place he one day hoped to retire to; he'd told his wife that with all the Londoners buying property in the county as second homes, and inflating Norfolk's house prices, global warming would have swallowed Norfolk up by the time he could afford a place.

In the centre of the circle was a photo of a young Sadie, binoculars draped around her neck. Among the books on procedure and law sat the odd British bird guide.

Through the window blinds the sun cast shadows across Rhodes's desk.

Colin Templeton was alone in the office. He wiped his brow, drops of sweat gathering at the nape of his neck and running down his back. It hadn't rained in weeks; while the start of the year had been Arctic, the last twenty-odd days had been the complete opposite.

DI Rhodes entered, carrying two polystyrene cups of water; he placed one on the desk in front of Colin. He then dodged the stacks of files on the floor and manoeuvred himself into his chair.

"So, you have some information for me."

Colin fidgeted excitedly, like a child.

"Oh, that I do!"

"You care to share it?"

Taking a sip of his water, Colin smiled; he was not going to give up his information without a little bit of game-play.

"How come you never got the DCI job?"

Rhodes stopped drinking and smiled at Colin. If he wanted to play games, Colin would need to be prepared to play hard.

"How come you never gave Abbie Flynn a lift Monday night?"

The reply knocked the grin off Templeton's face.

"Listen Colin, we both have information regarding this case. Difference is, my info puts you in jail for a long time and yours, well, it might just keep you out, so cut the shit and tell me what you know."

Rhodes was taking a risk showing his hand so quickly, but he'd never been one to keep his cards hidden long, especially if he felt he was holding a winning hand. People were going to find out sooner or later, so why not sooner?

"She walked away, said something about dropping her bracelet. After a few minutes I thought she'd gotten another taxi, especially when I saw that car reverse and then speed away."

Colin had Rhodes's attention again.

"A car?"

"Yep, silver Golf. Got the registration for you: Bravo, Victor, two numbers which I couldn't make out, then Charlie, Tango, Whiskey."

"Thank you – without the numbers, of course, we're looking at over a hundred matches. Still, something to go on with."

Rhodes went to speak, but was interrupted by his phone. It was Vilani. He listened as the constable explained what they'd found.

"One second, Tori. Excuse me for a minute, Mr. Templeton."

Rhodes got up and walked outside, leaving Colin alone.

Colin angled his head slightly as though he was looking at the pictures; however, he was really trying to catch the phone conversation.

Minutes later Rhodes returned and sat back down.

"Mr. Templeton, thank you for the information. I'll have it checked out."

"Is that it?"

"I'm afraid I have some bad news for you. A couple of my detectives visited your home this morning, and I'm sorry to inform you that they found your mother dead in her bed."

Nothing, not a flinch; it was as though Templeton hadn't actually registered the detective's words. Rhodes was expecting *something* – experience had taught him to expect some sort of response.

Then it came.

"What were detectives doing at my home?"

"Did you not hear me? Your mother has died."

"Who cares? About time; least now I know what that stench was."

Rhodes stood up and moved to the door. He opened it wide and looked back at Colin. "I think we're about done Mr. Templeton. I will, no doubt, be in touch. Go home and sort yourself out."

Templeton took his time to rise from the chair.

"Detective Inspector Rhodes: when you finish running the number plate details, if there's a car registered to a Mr. Alex Burns, I'd go there first. Then I'd go to the Railway Bridge pub and check to see if the manager's still waiting for his slapper of a daughter to come home."

Rhodes pushed his hand firmly against the exit door, shutting it tight to stop Templeton leaving.

"Why would I need to do that?"

Templeton's smile turned into a chuckle.

"Now I know why you didn't get the DCI post – you're not really very good at your job. I've worked with Burns; nasty piece of work. That Golf you'll be looking for is his."

Templeton pulled the door open as Rhodes loosened his pressure. The detective watched Templeton plod out towards the car park, where he stopped and turned around.

"Oh, nearly forgot: I also saw him bundling that pub manager's daughter into his taxi in Worcester last night."

Rhodes bound up the stairs to run the plate for matches.

There were sixty four in all; twelve in Kidderminster alone. One name stood out: Mr. Alexander J Burns, Hoo Road, Kidderminster.

Rhodes printed off the address, ran a second flight of stairs and placed the print-off on the desk in front of

Murray, who was readying himself for the trip to find Abbie Flynn's boyfriend.

"Change of plan. Check this address out for me."

Murray looked a little shocked.

"But Graham said –"

"Don't give a shit what Graham said; he put me in charge of this investigation."

"What about Toby Sinton?" Murray asked.

Rhodes spoke as he walked into his office, remerging with his suit jacket in his grip.

"Find out what Alex Burns was doing Monday night and where he was last night. Bates can chase the boyfriend alone; he has nothing to do with this – I'll put money on that. Graham is wrong. Joel, one thing I learnt a long time ago – good cops don't follow reporters, reporters follow good cops."

TWENTY-TWO

Joel Murray parked his car outside a townhouse built on the site of the old college. Five three-storey houses sat next to each other, identical in design in a way only modern architects know how to achieve.

The glossy black door, being so close to the roadside, had become aged by the traffic, and rattled as Murray knocked hard.

The door swung open instantly.

"What?"

"Good afternoon, I'm Detective Inspector Joel Murray. I was hoping to speak to a Mr. Alexander Burns."

The man's eyes widened. "Keep your voice down," he said, glancing up at the half-closed curtains of his neighbour's house.

"I take it you're Alex."

"Who else were you expecting to be in my house?"

Murray looked down at his notes. One read, 'Disappearance of Tammy Cavendish'.

"Well, that all depends who you were with last night."

"I'm on my way out," said Alex, stepping out of the house and closing the door softly.

Murray noticed the way he tried to do this without letting him see inside; it made it more apparent that Burns had something to hide.

Now that he'd come outside, Murray could see that Alex was wearing a grey body-builder's vest which just about covered his powerful upper body. Why do I always get the big ones? Murray asked himself.

Alex was now loading a bag into the back of his car.

"Going somewhere important?"

"The gym," Alex replied as he started to get in his car.

Murray put himself in front of the car door to stop Alex closing it.

"You work out? Now that does surprise me!"

"A comedian, are you?"

Murray made for his identification, "No, a police officer. I thought we already covered this. I just wondered how someone as busy as you gets time to go to the gym – you know, with work and hanging around stations and nightclubs."

Alex took the keys from the engine and stole another glance at one of his third floor windows and then the neighbours'.

"Someone you don't want to find out about my visit, right?"

"You work it out, you're the copper!"

"Okay, how's this. From the way you keep checking both your own and your neighbours' bedroom windows, you don't want people to see you speaking to a policeman, and from what's in the change holder there, you're hiding something from your wife."

Alex followed Murray's line of sight past him and into the space close to the gear stick, which contained some loose change, a Tesco Clubcard and a wedding ring.

"I'll talk, but not here. Meet me at AJ's at the back of the stadium."

"Bacon on crusty for me, and get them to put some of those world-class mushrooms on it, seeing as it's your shout."

Murray followed Alex closely, half expecting him to indicate into Stadium Close and then shoot off down the hill.

TWENTY-THREE

AJ's cafe was located on a barren industrial estate nearby and was home to an array of rusting corrugated units, long locked up and vacant. Any remaining businesses were only months, if not weeks, from being piled on the recession scrapheap.

In this sea of closed, roller-shuttered shacks the café sat like a filthy mirage. From the outside it looked like nothing special – hard to make an offensive shell of corrugated steel appear inviting. Even so, the café had a reputation for quality produce.

The interior was a cross between a bric-a-brac store and Aladdin's cave, but this was its appeal. It was different, unique. Among the mis-matched furniture, old-style advertising boards and personal pictures sat Detective Murray and Alex Burns.

Burns sipped casually from a steaming mug of coffee. Murray just watched. The cafe was compact. Even when it was busy, conversation was easily overheard. Joel spoke softly.

"So you wanted to talk?"

"No, I just wanted you away from my house," Alex said as he bit into a sandwich.

"Alex, I'm not stupid. You're not wearing your wedding ring – now that usually happens when someone's having an affair. None of my business, of course. But as you were leaving your own house, it seems to me..." Murray paused. "Correct me if I'm wrong with any of this. Your wife's away and you brought someone back last night who shouldn't have been there. Let's say, possibly, the daughter of a certain pub landlord."

Grinning, Murray took a bite from his sandwich.

Alex stayed quiet.

"Monday night your car was seen passing the station moments after an attack took place on a nineteen-year-old female. Did you see anything?"

Alex continued with his silence.

"I'll take that as a 'yes' then."

Alex moved his weight forward on to his elbows, pushing his face close to the detective's.

"How the hell is that a 'yes'?"

"Let me explain. You're hiding something, so that means your saw something. People don't hide things they didn't see – there's no need. So cut the crap and tell me what you saw."

Alex laughed aloud. "You pigs think you know everything. How about I explain something to you, fuckwit – my wife has gone away for the week and some slapper threw herself at me when I picked her up in Worcester last night, so I took a chance. I didn't realise adultery was police work now."

Murray's face tightened.

"I took my wedding ring off last night, like I do every time I go to the gym. I don't trust the people who look after the lockers there. Again, last time I checked, not a crime."

Alex scooped the last of his beans up into his mouth and rose. "For your information, my wife was driving the car on Monday night, I was out watching the football, and I was drinking. I don't drive when I drink, officer. That *is* a crime by the way. I'm going now, so settle the bill with the nice lady."

TWENTY-FOUR

"You like those books, then?" Daniel said, smiling at his son, whose head was buried in a book.

"Dad."

"I was only asking."

Ollie raised his eyes from the pages to give his father a look of disgust.

"I got this before school and I'm on chapter ten already; they're proper sick."

"And that's a good thing, I take it."

"Yeah, totally dank!"

Daniel looked down at his son. Sometimes it was like talking to an alien.

"Don't you have lessons and stuff to do at school? Like learning to speak English?"

"Dad!"

The boy opened the book at the page where he'd stuck his thumb and started to read again.

Partly, Daniel felt proud of the boy. At least he was reading and not glued to some phone or computer screen. On the other hand, he dreaded the future: the teenage strops, the drunken binges. The whole Ollie-growing-up thing scared Daniel to death.

"I was just wondering when you would get time to read nine chapters."

"It's easy – six at lunchtime and three just…" There was a tinge of frustration in the boy's voice as he shrugged.

Daniel indicated left and sat at the traffic lights on the Birmingham Road.

"Pizza for tea, if you like?"

"Love pizza!"

"Then there's some talk I would like to go to at the leisure centre."

Ollie folded the corner of the page he was reading and closed the book with a bang before placing it on the dashboard.

"Dad, really? You're joking, right?" Ollie looked suspicious, but more worried than anything else.

Daniel shook his head. "Thought you might be interested."

"No way, old man – not a chance."

"Does that book teach you to talk like that?"

Ollie just frowned.

"It's a talk by some writer, Mackenzie Rogers…"

"He writes these books!"

The book was thrust into Daniel's face; he struggled to push it away with one hand, the gold writing emblazed on its cover glinting in the sun: *Legend Of Gold: The Sovereign Select,* by Mackenzie Rogers.

Beyond the book cover, Daniel witnessed the smile that now lit up his son's face as he bounced around in his booster seat. A seat that he complained about being too big for every time he clambered into the car. This was the reaction Daniel had hoped for.

"Does he really? Lucky I got two tickets to tonight's book reading then."

"You're the best, Dad," said Ollie, followed by a mumbled, "I love you."

"You too, mate," Daniel replied, the warmth of his son's words flowing through him.

"Got the tent pitched up in the garden as well."

"Oh man, how did you learn to be such a great dad?"

"It's the only thing in life that comes naturally," Daniel replied, the words lost as his son became engrossed in his book again.

TWENTY-FIVE

The rear view mirror was angled so the entrance to the Morrisons car park was in clear view. Bates waited. Six lads had disappeared into the supermarket ten minutes earlier, and, as Bates expected, it didn't taken them long to reappear.

Toby Sinton, Flynn's boyfriend, was fourth from the front. The lad was at least six feet, with wavy, shoulder-length, chestnut-coloured hair; he wore flip-flops, a pair of pastel yellow shorts that flared out just below the knee and a grey t-shirt with some kind of Red Indian motif on it. Toby clutched a tray of lager under one arm and two large bags of crisps under the other. The group were all laughing as they jumped aboard a narrowboat that was moored not far from where the detective had parked.

Bates closed his car door and walked along a gravel track that ran alongside the river; as he approached the boat he took out his warrant card.

"DC Glenn Bates. I need a quick word with Mr. Toby Sinton."

Toby emerged from the far side of the boat. The group began to laugh and shout comments at the young lad.

Then Bates heard it, the sound of water bubbling. The engine began and the boat started to pull away from the bank slowly.

The detective weighed up his options: he could make a jump for it, but did he risk jumping aboard a boat with six young men who had no intention of stopping for him?

He stood still, watching as Toby Sinton pretended to surf as the boat moved off.

Bates knew what was going to happen; he had seen enough stag nights that had gone wrong back in Stourport to know what Toby Sinton had planned. He began to run back along the path toward a bridge upstream, much to the delight of the giggling audience on the boat.

Although age and fitness were against him, Bates got to the bridge at the exact moment he needed to. He bent down, a little breathless, adrenaline pumping, and waited the three seconds he calculated he would need.

As Toby's hands appeared at the edge of the bridge, Bates readied himself. He would let the lad pull himself up and get his balance – he didn't want him to fall backwards.

The lad's head followed his hands a second later, and he didn't even have time to land before Bates gripped him and pulled him down onto the cobbled street. He pushed his right knee hard into Sinton's ribs. The lad winced.

"I think we need a chat, my lad."

TWENTY-SIX

Bates's words did not raise DI Rhodes spirits; he'd guessed the boyfriend had no real connection, but had held out a little hope all the same. Toby Sinton was completely unaware of his girlfriend's situation and was at the present moment sitting in Glenn's passenger seat in a state of shock, awaiting a lift back to the hospital from a friend.

Rhodes thanked his colleague for the information and hung up.

On his desk sat a piece paper with five names written on it. The fourth name down was Toby Sinton; Rhodes took a pen and ran a line through it.

He studied the list for a few minutes, hoping something would jump off the page.

Daniel Stone, Alex Burns, Colin Templeton, Toby Sinton and underneath, with a large question mark at the end, Jakub Tesar. No matter what he thought, his eyes were drawn to the top name – Daniel Stone.

There was a tap on the door and Murray entered.

"Not him, boss – his wife was driving, but she's out of the country on holiday now. He's been a bit of a naughty boy – been playing away while she's gone, but other than being a complete prat there's nothing there."

Rhodes shook his head and exhaled loudly.

"Thanks, Joel, have a good night. I'll give you a call if we get anything over the weekend."

"Sure, Sir."

"Look after that wife of yours and let me know if we have a new member of the family before Monday."

*

The near constant need to itch his shins was becoming unbearable. There had to be some cream in one of his drawers. He opened then slammed them shut in turn. Five drawers and no cream – there were dozens of unused pens, a match programme from a Worcester Warriors rugby match (still unread), a lighter and reams of paper.

He stormed out of his chair and crossed the hall; he flinched from the sharp pin-prick sensation in his legs, and entered the men's toilets, making sure to push the door open with his elbow.

He never used his hands: hands carried germs, and not just handles but all surfaces. Knowing some of the men that used these toilets like he did, these doors carried more than the average. Rhodes had once seen a documentary about how the flu virus can be transported halfway around the world. He still remembered those grainy images of hospital wards full of sick and dying children.

Rhodes rested on the toilet seat and began to scratch. The pain was replaced with vibrating. He always sat on the toilet, door closed and his knees angled so they pointed at the door.

Public toilets were dangerous places. Nine times out of ten you didn't even have to time it right. You just used speed and brute force. You could rush in and a man would always be in a vulnerable position with hands in a place that left him unable to defend himself. A hand against the neck and your enemy's head would explode against the tiled wall. If the person you were after was clever enough to go into a cubical then it was human nature to stand. This would mean he had his back to a six foot door. The door would be easy to remove with the bottom of a foot. You could force your enemy to the floor with the door and there was always the porcelain toilet if you needed a surface to repeatedly bounce their head off. So, Rhodes always sat down. Prepared for anything. It was a problem, a habit that had grown so bad that it frustrated him every time he engaged in it, but he couldn't stop himself.

Rhodes's phone rang.

"Hi love, you having a good time?" He tried to sound cheerful through gritted teeth.

"Patrick, do you know anything about James getting into trouble?" his wife asked. She sounded worried.

Rhodes was utterly bemused.

"James?"

"Gemma's husband, you fool – her neighbour called and said he left the house this morning with who she thinks was a detective."

Patrick knew in an instant the reason the name Alex Burns had sounded familiar – his niece's husband. There was no way he could let her know what was going on.

"Nothing, sorry. Is Gemma with you?"

"No, she's in the shower."

He got up from the toilet and returned to his office.

118

"Can you ask her if she was driving by the station on Monday, about ten o'clock?"

The detective prided himself on being a good judge of character, and Alex James Burns, to his mind, was a menace. Just over ten years ago he had been on duty when a gang had attacked a young lad. Alex Burns – or James, as he liked to be known then – was the gang leader.

Burns, aged seventeen at the time, walked around the town thinking he was untouchable.

Rhodes proved he wasn't.

Burns ended up doing two years in prison, and nearly died in the process from a vicious knife wound to his wrist. Three years later Rhodes' worst fears were realised when his niece Gemma bought him home one Christmas Eve. Now he had to get on with him for Rita and Gemma's sake. Gemma had become more like a daughter to them than a niece, ever since her mother, his sister, had died of cancer ten years ago. He hated the way Alex looked at his niece and promised himself that the changed-man persona Alex portrayed would fall away, and that he would take great pleasure in being proven right when it did.

"Patrick, Monday is book club at Jenny's. If you got home on time you'd know what I get up to – we didn't leave until eleven, so she wouldn't have been anywhere near the station then."

Rhodes switched off his office light as he pulled on his jacket.

The journey home was quick. Hearing his wife jabbering on in her usual carefree manner about warm weather and the cocktails she was consuming at the poolside, reminded him of everything that was good. His wife, his daughter, and Gemma – the goodness in his life that illuminated the darkness he bore witness to every day.

No one would ever jeopardise that – something Alex Burns was about to find out.

TWENTY-SEVEN

Cigarette smoke drifted into the evening air, which, for the first time in two weeks, was cool. From a gap in the fire exit door, a dull glow stretched along an uneven, weed-infested pavement. Just beyond the light Mackenzie Rogers was enjoying the peace and his post-show smoke.

He loved his fans; they were paying the mortgage on his Victorian mansion in the Cotswolds, but readings came with some major drawbacks. The adult horror he wrote often attracted a strange fan base; some really freaked him out, wanting to talk in graphic detail about the murders and plot-lines. The children's book readings had just the one negative – severe headaches. Rogers often questioned whether it was the bright unnatural lighting the organisers always sat him under, or the sheer volume of children.

Tonight's event had been good, the children pleasant and inquisitive. He'd managed an hour of questions, which had saved him reading too much. So tonight he blamed the lighting instead of the children for his aching head.

Leaning against the outer wall of the leisure centre, he took another long drag, letting the smoke fill his cheeks before exhaling in an exaggeratedly slow motion. He scanned his surroundings and wondered what use this area was as a fire exit. Although at the end of the pavement there was a gate to the main road, getting to it through the wall of brambles could possibly inflict as much damage to the human body as a slight burn.

The nub of the cigarette fell to the floor and he ground it into the concrete before slurping from a mug of tea.

Rogers jolted at a sudden, loud bang. Maybe a car backfiring, he thought.

In an instant the pain in his head tripled, and his eyes twitched.

A warm fluid dripped down his cheek.

As his fingers brushed the hole in his temple his eyes closed. Slipping to the ground he realised he been shot, and that a bullet was lodged in the folds of tissue surrounding his brain.

He could feel his body shut down; his sight went and his ears sounded as though they were filling with water. There was a sweet smell, fruity aftershave maybe, not one he recognised.

"You should have listened," came a muffled voice from the darkness.

It was a male voice and he was close. Rogers felt the warmth of the man's breath against his cheek, then it all went cold.

TWENTY-EIGHT

Ollie jumped as the driver's door opened with a bang, dropping a bag full of books and signed photos. Seeing his dad clambering into the car juggling a can of pop, a pack of Smarties and a bag of crisps eased his fear.

"There you go."

Daniel placed the contents of his arms onto his son's lap, then carefully placed Ollie's rucksack onto the back seat.

"What was that bang?" asked the boy.

"What bang?"

Daniel *had* heard the bang, but, with the events of the weeks thus far, thought it best to get out of the car park as soon as possible.

"Was like a gun."

"It wasn't a gun, son – probably a car backfiring. They sound similar. Did you enjoy the reading and the signed stuff, mate?"

"It was great, Dad, thanks!" Ollie tucked into the Smarties and smiled.

"Can we eat the rest in the tent?" he asked.

"Sure." Daniel smiled, looking back to the road.

Daniel's mind took a few seconds to register the face, but once it did his body went cold. The face staring back at him through the glass of his rear view mirror was Jakub Tesar.

Tesar was just standing there, smiling.

Daniel's grip on the steering wheel tightened: a combination of fear and anger. He put his foot to the pedal, desperate to get away.

"DAD!"

Turning at the terror in Ollie's voice, Daniel managed to slam on his breaks, bringing the car to a screeching halt, inches from the thighs of a middle-aged man standing dumbfounded in the middle of the road.

"You okay?" Daniel said, jumping from the car.

"You could have killed me," the man said curtly.

Daniel didn't like the way he was being looked at.

"Do I know you? Your face is familiar," Daniel said, stepping away from the man.

"Taxi driver! People know your face but couldn't give a shit about your name, so long as you drive them to where they want to go."

"I don't take taxis. You sure I don't know you from somewhere else?"

The taxi driver didn't answer, just glared.

"I need to get my son home…" For the first time Daniel noticed the man's identification card, that hung on a cord around his neck. "Colin, you're sure you're okay?" He nodded at the ID card to indicate how he knew.

"Yeah."

The man strolled over to a taxi.

In all the fuss, Daniel had forgotten the reason for the near-miss.

Jakub Tesar.

The space he had been in was empty.

Daniel's heart sank.

Daniel opened his driver's door, dreading what he was about to see. To his surprise his son was still sitting there.

"Wow, Dad, that was so sick. Imagine if you had squashed him and his face was all mangled against our window."

"Let's get home; I think I need to speak to your mom on Sunday about your warped mind."

TWENTY-NINE

Neon blue, red, neon blue, red.

Colin found the lights on police cars hypnotic; a symbol of good. The light cutting through the darkness.

Colin often debated that choice of colour; to his mind blue was wrong, blue was cold; he thought that rescue vehicles' amber glow filled people with a warm, happy feeling, and that should be the colour of the emergency services too.

There were three sets of lights spinning slowly, illuminating the streets that surrounded the leisure centre. Two were in unison, the third, which blocked the street yards from where Colin Templeton had parked, was a fraction out of time.

He marked that down in a notepad with a knife-sharpened pencil. Colin was marking down everything he could see: the position of the police, the time the paramedics entered the complex, the various members of the crowd, trying to glean as much information as he could.

He visibly twitched with excitement, the type that fills a child on Christmas morning, or that of a teenage boy's first sexual arousal.

Three Bullets

A paramedic rushed from the entrance; she sprinted to the ambulance and threw open the back doors. Two more paramedics followed, pushing a stretcher on wheels. The sight of the patient sent Colin's heart racing – he knew him. Even through the oxygen mask and medical equipment he could see it was the famous writer Mackenzie Rogers.

Colin was half-expecting it to be just some stupid swimmer, but the presence of three police cars was a telltale sign that this was no ordinary incident, which was why he was waiting in the first place.

A celebrity killed in Kidderminster – that was something special. The strong chance of Rogers dying during the thirteen-mile trip to hospital made Colin smile. There were going to be hundreds of newspaper clippings to gather and TV reports to record and file. With his mother now taking up residence at the local morgue, he was free to record them without interference.

Struggling to see through the ever-darkening evening, Colin sketched faces from the crowd: a man with a beard; a young pregnant lady, paying attention to her hair, making sure the ringlets were exact. These pictures would be useful in his investigation. The nib of his pencil snapped halfway through drawing the left ear of a young lad on a BMX – a tap on the window had made him jump.

"You waiting for someone?" a policeman asked.

Colin was trying to think fast as he slammed the glove box closed.

"Had a call to pick up a Mr. Rogers; not shown though."

The policeman's eyes were fixed ahead as he knelt at the side of the car, which gave Templeton enough time to cover his notepad with a jumper.

The policemen rose and stepped away from the car, pulling out his radio and talking.

"John, that guy they've just loaded into the ambulance, what was his name?"

Colin waited while the policeman listened.

"Ok, thought so...yeah, thanks for that... Sorry, seems your fare hitched a lift elsewhere!" the officer smiled, pointing to the ambulance.

"Just my luck. Be on my way then."

Colin started his taxi and pulled away in a rush. He'd need to hurry if he was going keep up with that ambulance.

SATURDAY: DAY 5

THIRTY

A fresh cup of tea, firmly gripped; the sound of birdsong, the scent of dew. The world was a different place for Daniel in the early morning sunshine – that feeling that a new day lay ahead, a fresh start.

He relaxed on an ancient garden bench, its once green wood finish brittle and decaying now. Daniel loved the bench. He loved just sitting in his garden watching clouds drift, knowing that all the curtains on the surrounding houses were drawn and most, if not all of the occupants were sleeping.

Soon, the hum of twenty-odd lawnmowers and the hiss of numberless hosepipes would interrupt this morning bliss, followed by the gleeful screams of children playing and the constant contraction of springs as the trampoline brigade commenced.

Two doors down there lived two boys, around six and eight. They had a trampoline which took up most of their garden. A big, netted, blue enclosure. They may as well have been birds, they spent so much time in the air.

He hadn't planned to wake so early, but several drops of condensation thudding against his forehead made an effective alarm clock. Sleeping wasn't easy recently. There were so many thoughts pressing. On reflection, the previous evening's six hours seemed something of an accomplishment. Considering Ollie's near two-hour excited explanation of the plot of the book he was reading and the two previous installments, any sleep at all was a bonus. Through the tent's opening, Daniel watched Ollie sleep; he was stretched out, star-like, on an airbed, his Star Wars sleeping bag draped over his lower body.

Daniel took another gulp of sugary tea, warm in his throat.

He took in the garden – it needed work. Months of neglect were taking their toll on the once well-tended flowerbeds. This garden had been a constant presence. He played here as a child; he and Natalie had drunk champagne here to celebrate purchasing the property from his parents. On this very bench Natalie had accepted his marriage proposal, and the circle was completed by Ollie's playing where he himself once played.

Scanning the garden now, he was filled with dread at a memory he wished he could erase. The only sadness that this tranquil environment had ever witnessed now wounded him once more. He forced himself to look at the back door; it was there he had listened to his wife talking through her plans to leave him for her lover.

Another image came to confuse him; there was a lady standing in front of him, then, like the flicker of candle before being extinguished, she was gone. Out of the corner of his eye he saw the figure appear in the upstairs window. Daniel snapped his head back around.

He hadn't expected it. To see her face again in their house – what used to be their house anyway – after all these years? That sweet smile. That sweet, disingenuous smile that he had always thought showed love. A smile that was no more than a ghost now.

How long was it? Six years?

Six long years since he discovered that she'd been deceiving him. Since she left him. Half a dozen years to get over the pain, the betrayal; to build a new life.

Daniel had tried to forget. He'd tried to build that life, and on the brink of his greatest failure, on the brink of leaving that old life behind, she was back, standing at the window, her hair immaculate, her make-up pristine, just as she'd always been.

Fighting reason, he smiled.

She waved and disappeared.

THIRTY-ONE

Before Daniel could rise to his feet, Natalie appeared at the back door, her index finger beckoned him toward her.

She cut an elegant figure as she leaned against the door frame and her white maxi-dress, decorated with large red poppies, floated softly around her.

"What's going on?" Daniel said, rushing to her side.

"Inside, I don't want Ollie to know I'm here."

"Why are you here?"

Natalie looked away, trying to hide her embarrassment.

"Come on, Nat – there has to be a reason for you to just turn up here after six years."

"Tom and I had a disagreement and this was the only place I wanted to be. So I came last night, just to talk, but you were out."

"So you broke in?"

"No! I still have a key. I watched you and Ollie come home. You looked so happy, and when you went straight to the tent, I just sat and watched you both until you switched off the torch and I fell asleep. It was just like old times. It made me happy."

This was not what Daniel wanted to hear – the last six years of his life had been a painful struggle as he tried to recover from his failed marriage.

"It's nice to see you happy again, getting on with life."

Getting on with life? Was that what she really saw?

Daniel wanted to tell her just how his life really was, how bad it had been. How much he'd longed, over the past six years, to have his old life back. It may have been mundane – the repetitive cycle of work, dinner, baths and bed – but that was exactly what he'd loved. Daniel enjoyed the cosy predictability of that life. But that same predictability had ended his marriage and torn his son away. Anger built inside him but, predictably, Daniel did not tell Natalie any of this.

"So what now?"

"I'm going to go; I need to speak to Tom. It was a stupid argument, and we need to sort it out."

Emptiness consumed Daniel again. He went to hold her hand, but his son screaming his name from the garden arrested his attention.

"Go check on him, Dan."

"Stay here, I'll be right back."

Daniel turned to the door and ran to the tent.

He glanced back to the kitchen – she was gone.

THIRTY-TWO

Four rows in front and six seats across; that should be far enough away yet close enough to keep an eye on him. When choosing his seat, Rhodes made sure there were enough people of average size between him and his target; in this way the view he had of Alex Burns was in part covered. He didn't mind Alex seeing him – just not yet. A few minutes of observation was what Rhodes needed first, just to get a feel for his behaviour.

A loud cheer rang around Sixways Stadium as the local rugby team took to the field. Alex Burns clambered to his feet and clapped, trying in vain not to spill any of his lager. Rhodes remained seated, his eyes fixed on Alex. Rugby was the one indulgence that remained in Rhodes's life. No time for bird-watching any more, and even rugby was beginning to take a back seat. But today he could combine both.

An hour and a half passed quickly and, before Rhodes knew it, people were leaving their seats and heading for the exits. The game hadn't registered; instead he'd spent the last ninety or so minutes starring at Alex Burns's profile.

Now he rushed to keep his eyes trained on the back of Burns's head as it cut through the buoyant crowd. He was disappearing; Rhodes was tall, but there were just too many bodies between them. He was gone.

Once out of stadium and into the open space of the car park, the crowd dispersed, but there was still no sign of Alex. Angry at his failure, Rhodes made his way back to his car.

"You trying to follow me, old man?" Alex asked, approaching Rhodes from behind.

Rhodes spun to face him.

"Following's for sheep. I get what I want to come to me," he replied.

"Looked like you gave up to me."

"All part of the game."

The men took a few paces toward each other, the way stags do before crashing heads.

"So, I'm here, what do you want? I take it it's not to say hello."

"Just checking up on you."

"I'm honoured."

A smile broke out across Alex's face, as the pair now mirrored each other's movements.

"If I was you I'd be worried; a man like me paying you attention can only mean bad things," said Rhodes.

"Do you want to borrow my phone?"

"What for?"

"Well, if you've come for a fight you may want to ring some friends."

"Just because you pump yourself full of steroids doesn't mean I won't beat you senseless." Rhodes leaned forward and his hand meet Alex's chest. "A warning, Alex –

when Gemma comes home you'll be gone. There will be a note – get a friend to write it if you still struggle with that."

Alex pushed Rhodes's hand away.

"Threats like that nearly got you killed last time. How is the arm?"

Rhodes didn't speak. He never moved his gaze from the man in front of him. He reminded himself of the scar his shirt now hid. It was thin, long and circled three-quarters of his wrist. It was over ten years old but still it itched. His body's reminder not to make rash decisions.

"Walk away, Alex – while you still can!"

"Maybe I will. I could walk up to Sadie; bet she'd be happy to see me."

Rhodes pounced in one movement, slamming Alex against the side of a grey Ford Puma. It dented a little on the wing. He floored Alex and used his knee, bringing it hard into his ribs.

"Listen to me now! I will get you, one way or another!"

Alex lay there silent.

"The best outcome you can wish for is prison."

"You're going to be in big trouble for this. I might drive a taxi but that doesn't make me stupid."

"No, your piss-poor IQ makes you stupid!"

Rhodes watched Alex get back to his feet, willing him to try something, hoping for a reason to give him a few more blows.

Alex smiled, brushed himself down and began to walk toward his car.

"You're a police officer – try to remember that."

Rhodes was fishing his keys from his pocket just as Alex swung his right arm. His reaction time was a little slower than normal, but Rhodes managed to lift his left arm to block. The contact came somewhere in between his wrist and his elbow; he forced Alex's arm away and at the same time swung a right.

The contact knocked Alex backward.

There was blood on Rhodes's knuckles; he'd still been holding his car keys and had subconsciously gripped the largest key in between his fingers. The key had pierced Alex's face, just underneath the cheekbone.

"People don't get away with hurting my family," said Rhodes as he stared at Alex, half expecting more punches.

They never came.

THIRTY-THREE

The evening was pleasant; a mixture of reds and oranges scrawled across the sky.

Roberts and Crooks walked slowly toward the Templeton's old caravan. In the distance, the daylight began to disappear behind the tree line of the Wyre Forest. As far as the eye could see, evergreens stretched to meet the coming dusk.

The caravan park was busier than it had been on their last visit. There were a lot of weekend owners and the small sports field was filled with children. A football flew across the road. Crooks trapped the ball under his foot, moved it back and forth a couple of times and then passed it back to a fair haired boy who looked on unimpressed.

"You enjoyed that, didn't you?"

"What?"

"Trying to show off in front of the kids."

The two detectives passed the onsite Social Club, nodding to a few smokers outside before they approached the Templeton residence.

Roberts knocked.

Colin Templeton opened the door, dressed in nothing more than a worn pair of boxer shorts. From inside came a waft of vinegar and then fish – in that order of intenseness.

Roberts looked up, her eyes level with Templeton's crotch.

"DS Roberts and DC Crooks. Could we have a word?"

"No."

"Would you mind putting some clothes on, sir?"

"I'm perfectly comfortable with what I'm wearing. If you're not, you could always remove some. Now that would be a fun way to start a conversation."

Jackie Roberts was not fazed; she'd been in the force long enough to have dealt with all kinds of people and all kinds of attitudes. She was also extremely stubborn, something she got from three generations of powerful female role models.

"I'm fine as I am. The conversation won't take long," she added.

"No, it won't – it won't take you long to turn around and go away."

Templeton went to close the door; Crooks put his body in the way.

"Mr. Templeton, we're aware that your mother died early this week." Crooks tried to sound sympathetic.

Templeton just looked at them. "So am I."

"I cannot begin to understand the effect your mother's death has had on you."

Templeton remained silent.

"Sir. We have had a report that you may have been in the property at the time of her death."

"I was; so?"

"So, if it's okay with you we need to ask you a few quick questions." Crooks was half expecting a 'no' answer and more force needed to stop the door closing. Instead, Templeton spoke.

"Billy Big Bollocks sent you, has he? Keep an eye on the weirdo eyewitness."

"Sorry, sir, it won't take a minute," Roberts said.

"Listen, she was a pain in the ass, she just lay there, nothing wrong with her, and if you want the truth, I'm pretty glad she's gone. I can live my life now. Fourteen, that's how old I was when she took my life from me, fourteen – and she got lazier and lazier. I cooked for her, washed her. You ever had so much shit underneath your nails that even the fourth scrub with a brush won't release it?"

There was no response. Crook glanced over his shoulder; it seemed their presence was attracting attention from some of the noisier residents. Five of the children from the park stood at the bottom of plot, watching. In the middle was the little fair haired lad, his ball tucked under his arm.

Templeton continued to talk. "No, I don't suppose you have. It stopped me biting my nails, that's for sure. I was here when she died, however, I had no idea that she *was* dead – I've lived with her stench so long I've gotten used to it."

"Did you check on her before you left for work?" asked Roberts.

"No. I left everything she needed on her bed the night before. She didn't like me going in in the morning in case I woke her."

"Okay, sir, we're sorry to bother you, and sorry for your loss."

They turned to walk away, but Templeton emerged out of his home for the first time. He waved his fist angrily at the children.

"Go on you little bastards, go and tell your drunken excuses for parents that the strange man killed his mom and ate her."

The children ran. Crooks gave Templeton a long stare before leaving.

"So you two are sorry? Good! How about you apologise for disturbing my evening?"

"Certainly sir, we apologise for disturbing you. Have a good night," Roberts said.

As they walked back toward their car Crooks asked Roberts what she thought.

Her answer was short: "A creep."

THIRTY-FOUR

No matter how many times he read the text, the words didn't change.

C U at 8
T
X

    Alex Burns was regretting Thursday night more than any he could remember in his life. Coming to Tammy Cavendish's aid was stupid; there had been some fantastic sex, but the last thing he needed was the teenage daughter of a local hardman hanging around a few days before his wife was due back from holiday.

    Tonight he was going to tell Tammy Cavendish where she stood: it had been a one night thing, a mistake – an enjoyable mistake, but there was no more to it, nothing else to follow.

    If she got upset, so be it – she was young. She'd have plenty of years ahead to get used to being treated like a piece of meat. She had a good body and an open mind, so it was bound to happen. Give it ten years and she would be begging for this type of attention when age started to become a female's enemy.

The doorbell rang.

Alex glanced at the clock: 7:59. The option not to reply, in the hope she would take the hint, had failed.

He strode to the door, every step increasing the adrenaline that pumped through his body, fuelling his rage. He was just going to tell her, there on the doorstep, that he'd made a mistake, that he was happily married. It was possible she would be okay with this and leave…there was also the chance that she would take it badly and tell her dad. If her father found out he would no doubt use violence to protect his daughter – something Alex would have to deal with if and when the occasion presented itself. Fear was never an option for Alex Burns.

"Listen, you slut," he shouted, opening the door.

A flustered elderly lady greeted him.

"Sorry…"

"Well, I knew he liked them young, but he never told me he liked to shag grannies as well. I hope you've saved some spunk for me," Tammy said, brushing past the horrified lady.

Alex pushed Tammy inside; he apologised to his bemused neighbour and slammed the door shut.

Tammy looked at his bruised cheek, the skin around the puncture point swollen and intensely red. It looked uncomfortable.

"Someone been a naughty boy?"

He brushed it with his fingers. "You need to go and not come back."

Alex's words were lost on Tammy; she was examining his worldly possessions. A large TV, random jade ornaments everywhere, floral jade cushions, placed at perfect intervals on a long brown sofa – not the usual bachelor pad décor. Thursday, when she was here, with the lights off and engrossed in ripping at Alex's clothes, the closest she got to the living room was the carpet on the stairs.

She looked confused, as though trying to take everything in.

A photo of Alex in a suit next to a very attractive brunette lady in a wedding dress came into view.

She began to breathe hard.

"Tell me she's your sister,"

Alex smiled on seeing she was hurt; he felt in control.

"It doesn't matter who she is, does it?"

"I may be some things, Alex, but I don't do married men."

"You did Thursday, and I bet you would drop your knickers like a hooker if I asked. That is if you have any on."

Alex moved to grab her arm to throw her out.

Tammy swung her free hand – no warning, just the flat of her hand hard against his cheekbone. It caught him off guard and he recoiled in shock. A slap hard enough to split capillaries has that effect, even more so when the skin is already wounded.

The pair paused, working out what was about to happen.

Alex touched his face; it smarted half from pain, half from embarrassment. He jerked forward; not far, but far enough for Tammy to know what she needed to do.

She was small and no match for his bulk; his sheer size would knock her flat on her back, which was in one way what she wanted.

The second before he made contact she pushed her weight onto her heels, allowing herself to fall backward before she was forced. Her backside hit the floor first, then her back, which jarred her neck a little. The second between their falls gave Tammy just enough time to bring her knee toward her abdomen.

The mass of Alex's body came down on top of her like a train hitting a stationary car on a level crossing. She felt as though her chest was being demolished from the outside. The pain was more or less what she expected, but lasted a few seconds more than she would have hoped for. She drew a long breath.

Then she heard what she was waiting for – a cry like that of a wounded animal – and the weight above her lifted.

Alex rolled in agony, his hands clenched between his legs. A sound like a deflating bagpipe echoed around the magnolia walls.

Tammy rose from the floor; her body ached, but she laughed, proud of how her father's training had left her muscular aggressor writhing on the floor. You don't grow up the only daughter of Mark Cavendish not knowing how to look after yourself. That was lesson number one.

"You're going to regret this," she gasped.

Alex squinted through watery eyes.

"Slappers like you are all the same. You're like the first piece of bread in the bag – you know, a little thicker than the others, everybody touches it at some point but no-one actually really wants it. Go home, tell Daddy that sleeping around got his slag of a daughter in trouble."

Tammy planted her foot into Alex's mouth, splitting his lip like a cheap teabag.

Three Bullets

"He'll never find out about this, or the cops might find out about what you were doing on Monday night with that girl."

Alex froze.

"Nothing to say? Didn't think you would have."

With that, she left.

SUNDAY: DAY 6

THIRTY-FIVE

"You ready to order, sir?"

The waitress's words dragged Rhodes from his daydream; he had been focusing on a minute ripple in the otherwise calm water of the canal. The waterway ran parallel to a small wooden picket fence that separated a grass verge from the beer garden of The Watermill pub. Rhodes was not enjoying his time off; with his wife on holiday, dining alone was turning into more thinking time about his failure to make progress on the Abbie Flynn case.

"Can I have the surf and turf please?"

The waitress wrote down his order.

Rhodes noticed then that she was beautiful and immaculately turned out; she couldn't have been more than eighteen, but had an air of sophistication beyond her years. He smiled with something akin to a proud father's warmth.

"How would you like your steak, sir?"

"Medium rare, please, and could I have it with veg rather than salad."

"Certainly, sir."

Rhodes watched her walk away and gave another smile. Her whole life ahead of her, just like his daughter. His smile faded as he finished the thought: unlike Abbie Flynn.

A child screamed from the small climbing frame as her father dragged her away to eat her dinner. This amused Rhodes; he remembered such battles with his own daughter. You didn't have to be a scientist to figure out that trying to get a child to eat a plate of food while watching other children playing wasn't going to be easy.

The food, when it came, was good. He buried his knife deep into the steak and cut a sizeable piece before pushing it onto his fork with half a piece of scampi. A fantastic combination of tender steak with the texture of the breadcrumbs and the softness of the fish filled his mouth.

He sat back from the table and enjoyed the moment; the sight of two children leaning against the fence waving at a passing narrowboat added to his warmth of feeling.

His phone vibrated in his pocket and he looked at the display: DS Roberts.

"Jackie."

"Sorry to bother you on a Sunday, Patrick. Got some info you might want to hear. You know I'm working on Friday's shooting investigation? Well, the victim was children's writer Mackenzie Rogers."

Rhodes placed his knife and fork down, "I know, it's all over the news."

"Mackenzie Rogers is just a pen name; his real name is Roger Mackenzie."

"Bet it took him a while to come up with that."

Roberts took no notice. "Well, Roger is CEO of Ryadim Plastics."

"So?"

"Ryadim Plastics are a London-based company; they have a sales and distribution centre in Birmingham."

Rhodes was struggling to see any connection, but he'd worked with Roberts for long enough to know that she wouldn't interrupt his precious day off for no good reason.

"Is there a point, Jackie? My steak is going cold."

"Steak beats my Mars bar. Ryadim Plastics were the employers of one Daniel Stone – that was until Roger Mackenzie fired him on Monday."

The half-loaded fork dropped to his plate.

"You in the office?"

"Will be in a minute, just on the way over from the mortuary."

"See you there in five."

Rhodes took another mouthful of food.

"You're not working today," said Roberts.

"Am now!"

Rhodes disconnected and rushed from his seat, leaving half a plate of food behind.

THIRTY-SIX

Six-thirty in the evening, nearly twenty-four hours since Tammy's threat of exposure, and Alex was waiting by the door, suitcase in hand, mulling over what to do next.

His life had radically changed since he'd met Gemma.

The old gang had tried hard to get him involved in the life he used to live. It was easy to say no; their gaunt, acne-ridden faces were an automatic reminder of where he could be. Only two weeks ago he'd seen Stevie Taylor hanging aimlessly around the bins in the town centre, on the hunt for some sort of fix. He'd gone home and made love to Gemma just to shake the image.

He was at a crossroads.

The devil stood with him.

The devil wore a fine suit and looked like Patrick Rhodes.

The devil spoke.

He asked what Alex wanted from life. Alex answered: to make Gemma happy. The devil laughed and said, it's too late for that. The devil laughed again. You have one choice: how sad do you want to make her? That's what you need to decide.

Alex was back in his living room.

The devil was full of shit. Gemma was going to be sad, very sad indeed.

Did he do what Rhodes wanted and leave?

Did he hell!

Some people ran from trouble, and others stood their ground. Alex always stood his ground, no matter what, even when this meant ending up in prison like it had last time he and Rhodes had drawn swords.

He actually relished the thought of coming head-to-head with Rhodes again.

Tammy couldn't have seen what happened Monday night – he would have been under arrest already if she had. Someone must have seen him there and told the police; that's why they sent that detective around earlier in the week.

Alex tried hard to remember who could have possibly seen him, and then it hit him, about as hard as Tammy's knee had.

"You little inbred bastard, I'm going to torch your tin house."

That weirdo he used to work with, Templeton! That was who he'd seen running away from the station Monday night. He should've remembered his face the day after, when he saw him in the window of the pub. He'd been too occupied with his own worries to think straight. He was thinking straight now though, as Templeton was about to find out.

He glanced at his wedding day picture. It was too late for her to start finding out. It was all about taking as many people down on his way back to prison as he could.

THIRTY-SEVEN

Turning right off the main road into his street, Daniel could see an Audi parked parallel to his house. The closer he got the clearer DI Rhodes became.

By the time Daniel exited his car, the detective was standing where the pavement joined Daniel's driveway.

"DI Rhodes, you okay?"

Rhodes waited at the edge of the driveway, waiting to be invited on to Daniel's property.

"I'm good, thank you. Good weekend?"

Rhodes had come for more than a pleasant chat, and Stone knew it.

"Busy, very busy. Spent a lot of quality time with my lad. Can I help you?"

"You sure can. I need to ask you a few more questions. Can we go inside?"

Rhodes waited for a sign that Daniel was okay with his request. Daniel left the front door open, which seemed about as much of an invite as Rhodes could have hoped for.

The two men sat in the living room, in the exact same positions Tesar and Daniel had sat early that week. Daniel shuddered as he realised this.

Rhodes held a cup of tea Daniel had made, and there was a small plate of biscuits on the arm of the chair.

Rhodes scanned the living room – it was clean and tidy. This did not surprise him at all. A man who offered tea and biscuits to a policeman would be quite at home with housework. Not just a policeman either, but one that, in all honesty, was trying his hardest to pin not one but two attacks on him.

There was a swimming bag lying against the wall and a towel darkened by water hanging up to dry. An Aston Villa match programme, the corner bent back, sat next to him on the carpet near the TV.

"You have been busy. Swimming, football – your lad spending your redundancy money already?" Rhodes smiled.

Daniel stayed quiet.

"Mr. Stone, I've been through your statement again. In it you said there was a gunman on the platform on Monday night."

Daniel went to reply, but Rhodes continued.

"Well, on Friday night, we believe this gunman may have been operating within the Kidderminster area. You're description of this man was sketchy – is there anything more you remember about him? Maybe you've seen him around since Monday?"

Pausing for a beat, Daniel wrestled with his conscience. Tell the policeman everything and he could be killed; the alternative, tell him nothing and it could be jail.

"I've told you everything I can remember, sorry."

"Well, if he does try to contact you, then let us know straight away."

"Why would he contact me?"

Rhodes sensed Daniel's nervousness from across the room.

"I don't mean to scare you, but this Czech man seems to have a connection to you; we don't know how yet, but we will find out. The person we believe he shot was also connected to you, and we're worried he could come after you next."

"My boss?"

"Roger Mackenzie, yes. You are aware of the shooting?"

"Who isn't? It's national news. He was a famous man, and a good friend. It must have been five minutes after we'd left that he was killed. My son said he heard a gunshot but I told him it must have been a car back-firing."

Rhodes edged forward in his chair.

"You were there?"

"I took Ollie to Mr. Mackenzie's book signing – he's a massive fan."

Daniel forced his next words out, trying to erase any dishonesty in his tone. "Mr. Mackenzie was still in the hall when we left."

Rhodes's eyes were drawn to Stone's left hand; there was a tan-line just above the knuckle. The background information had said that Stone had split up with his wife six years ago, so the appearance of the line baffled Rhodes.

"When did you get back from holiday, Mr. Stone?"

"Last Saturday. I had two weeks in Lanzarote. Why?"

"You miss your wife?"

Stone was stunned; the question was intrusive and he felt threatened. "What?"

"You miss her? She left you for another man, is that correct?"

"She left me, yeah, but she met the other man after...I don't see where this is going, Inspector."

There was a silence while Rhodes thought what to ask next.

"Did it take you long to get over her?"

"A couple of months – what is this, *Mastermind*? My specialist subject: the split of Mr. and Mrs. Stone."

"Hard times, I expect."

"Detective Rhodes, I was in a dark place then – my life was not my own. I missed my wife, I missed my son. You're married – imagine how you'd feel if she walked out on you."

"It would kill me, but the first thing I'd do if I knew it was over, I mean really finished, no-going-back over, would be to remove my wedding ring and get rid of it. So, can you answer why, six years on, you have a tan-line that tells me that, until recently, let's say a week ago for argument's sake, you were still wearing your wedding ring?"

"Really, you'd just throw away your ring? You know that for sure, do you? I think maybe a man like you would fight hard to keep something he needed. It may seem strange to you, but I had my reasons for keeping my ring."

The pair watched each other hard. Daniel sat still; Rhodes took a custard cream from the plate and dunked it.

"Enlighten me. I like strange. I spend a lot of time around strange."

"I moved on, but not enough. Taking my ring off for good would have ended a life I didn't want to leave behind. Then things seemed to be picking up. I was told to take a holiday before an interview for a new position. I was excited for the first time in a long time. The day before I flew home, I threw the ring into the sea and prepared for a new start."

"And then you returned and your life didn't improve; it got worse. Tell me, was there any point during the last six years when you felt like it was too much, like it was never going to get better, like your only option was to take the coward's way out and end it all? Maybe last Monday night, perhaps."

There was another silence.

"It never crossed my mind, not once," said Daniel. "My son kept me going: the thought of seeing him at the end of every week kept me strong. Also, suicide should never be seen as a coward's way out, Detective Rhodes. In my opinion it's the bravest thing a person can do."

"Brave!"

"The most important thing you have in your life is life itself. Your family, your friends, your gleaming Audi…they're only there because you are alive. To take all that away takes guts. I know I'd never have been strong enough to do that."

"So you think it's brave to take a life?"

"No, I think it's brave to take your *own* life. To take someone else's is as low as a human being can stoop." Stone got up and headed into the hall. Opening the front door, he turned to Rhodes. "I think you should leave now."

Rhodes took the hint.

"Thank you, Mr. Stone – and remember, if he does contact you, please get in touch."

Rhodes was halfway over the threshold when he spotted the shadow of the back door from the corner of his eye. The door swung half open and then slammed shut in the wind.

"Did you know your back door's open, Mr. Stone?"

Daniel turned to look. "Kids, hey – Ollie never closes it behind him."

"Be careful, Mr. Stone. Anyone could get in."

THIRTY-EIGHT

The car was still there, just parked on the street outside the house; it had been half an hour since they'd spoken.

What did he want?

Why wasn't he out looking for Tesar?

Daniel did feel some small sense of relief. After all, if the police were camped outside his house, then Tesar would hardly come back.

Daniel closed Ollie's bedroom door. Its contents hidden for another week, he stood motionless for a few seconds, listening to the sounds of the house. A bath was running across the landing and the TV was just audible from downstairs – the house was quiet.

Daniel hated Sunday evenings. Most people disliked Sunday evenings, but for Daniel there was deep regret. Time had moved so fast and he hadn't made the most of his time with Ollie, and it was too late to make it right. Added to this was the fact that Sunday evenings were a twilight before the weekend disappeared and the working week began again. Tonight, though, he didn't have the usual Monday blues: tomorrow was the first Monday morning since he'd been fired. No work and Ollie gone; the thought left a sort of emptiness that ached inside him.

He threw a white bath towel into the bathroom and stepped into his bedroom to undress.

Daniel crossed the landing and stepped into the bath. Freezing. He was sure he'd turned the hot tap on. He shivered.

From outside came the bang of a car door. Rhodes was leaving.

Clutching a towel, Stone went to the front of the house and peered out onto the street. Rhodes was nowhere to be seen, but the car was still there. Maybe he was off for a toilet break or to get some tea from the chip shop, or just a quick walk to stretch his legs. One thing was clear: Rhodes was in no rush leave Daniel alone.

It took ten minutes to re-fill the bath; soft bubbles floated around Daniel's neck, and, at last, he relaxed. Warm water rolled across him like the tide as he took deep breaths.

His eyes focused on one of the three ceiling spotlights, and his mind drifted to his son's smile on Friday night as they camped, their laughter while swimming and his excitement watching the football.

He closed his eyes tight and submerged his body; the water rose above the overflow and spilled over the sides, leaving tiny puddles on the floor. Only his nose rose above the water.

In those relaxed moments under the water, Daniel Stone made a decision.

Life was shit, but shit had its uses – plants thrive in it.

Daniel needed to plant a new life, to watch it grow; that would start with a job – any job would do – that would be the seed. But first, he decided to take care of Jakub Tesar.

He needed somewhere quiet; not far away, but far enough to sort out the reason behind the recent events.

Water dribbled into his mouth as he smiled beneath the water.

He was still smiling as he pushed his head above the water-line.

From downstairs there was a thud. Daniel swallowed deeply. He knew the noise; it was the back door shutting.

A couple of minutes passed silently. Fear stopped Daniel opening his eyes. He no longer expected to be alone in his bathroom. He took one deep breath and opened his eyes.

The room was empty.

Daniel grabbed his towel and reached for the door. It hit him full in the face, and he fell backwards.

A hand gripped his neck and pushed his head back under the water.

THIRTY-NINE

Puddles of water became lakes and water cascaded over the side of the bath as Daniel's arms windmilled in a desperate effort to strike his attacker.

Forcing his eyes open, he gulped for air; it took all his effort to slump over the bath, his arms dragging along the floor.

His ribs ached, and with every breath, he let out a wheeze.

He was alone.

Daniel forced himself from the bubbles and winced as his feet touched the floor. Clutching his ribs, he crossed the landing and into his bedroom.

He slipped a pair of jeans over his wet legs and cautiously went down the stairs.

The TV was still on, and Daniel thought it sounded louder than before. As his foot touched the second to last step, his attacker came into view.

Jakub Tesar was sitting, remote in hand, in Daniel's living room.

"You piece of shit!"

Jakub didn't even turn his head.

"I take it you don't want the job, then?"

Daniel couldn't see Tesar's right hand, so he took no chances, moving slowly into the room in case the gun was within reach.

"I want you out of my house."

"You want out of our game?"

"You think this is a game? A man is dead, and a young girl is dying."

Tesar switched the TV off; he coughed. Daniel glimpsed his face. He was smiling.

"Let me explain to you what a game is. It's a competitive activity involving skill, chance, or endurance on the part of two or more persons who play according to a set of rules, usually for their own amusement or more often for the amusement of spectators. What we're fucking about at does seem, to me, to be a game.

"Daniel, you're right – a man is dead, and not just any man; a well-respected, professional, family man, who from all reports, was loved by just about everyone who'd crossed his path. Why is this man dead?" Tesar stood up and turned slowly to face Dan.

"Because you killed him!"

"Wrong, Daniel. You're to blame. There are approximately seven billion people on this planet, and ninety percent are just a fucking drain on resources, of no real value to the human race, but you choose a man who in the last twelve months alone gave nine million to charity just to try to help these fucking runts out. How does that make you feel?"

Daniel answered by rushing his intruder, but Tesar moved as though expecting the attack. Daniel crashed onto the floor.

Daniel clambered to his feet and watched Tesar amble into the hallway. His back was turned, which Daniel saw as another chance and charged again. Still too slow. Bone crunched against the wall as Daniel's cheekbone ripped open.

"Don't be fucking stupid! You're in pain. Now stop, before it kills you, you know you don't want that." Jakub looked at his victim, at the blood pouring from his face. He took hold of him and jerked him to his feet. "You remember the second name you gave me?"

Daniel was clearly dazed.

"I'm still going to kill them, but I'm going make it hurt more than the first because of your silly attempts at being a bastarding hero!"

Looking deep into Tesar's eyes, Daniel tried to catch him off guard, throwing his head forward; it landed directly on the bridge of Tesar nose. The grip on his wrists eased in an instant. Daniel threw a punch with his right hand, but his attacker was already falling. The punch missed and came to rest firmly against the door frame, cracking Daniel's knuckles.

He screamed out in pain.

There was a bang at the door. Daniel fell to his knees. Tesar struggled to his feet and staggered towards the kitchen.

"Stone, are you okay?" Rhodes shouted through the letterbox.

"Help!" Lying on his back now, Daniel watched as Rhodes smashed into the front door, the third attempt taking the door off its hinges.

"It was him." Rhodes checked the downstairs rooms and ran through to the kitchen. The back door was open.

Rhodes returned to Daniel, who he could see was badly injured. He called for an ambulance. "You'll be okay," he said. "We'll catch this guy."

Daniel closed his eyes, and felt they might never open again.

FORTY

The human hand has one major purpose: grip.

Sandra Flynn used her hands now to their fullest potential in squeezing her daughter's pale blue hand. Indeed, her knuckles whitened with the pressure of it. Around her, the bed sheets were damp with tears.

Her make-up was in need of restoration; dried tears etched mascara-lined tracks into her foundation. She was almost unrecognisable.

Sometimes, a week can fly by; not this week, not for the Flynn family. As May neared and with it summer, Sandra foresaw only pain.

Their planned July holiday to the Maldives only held a fleeting thought, which was only the need for it to be cancelled.

Across the room she watched her husband's hand also working hard, gripping a pen.

In his line of work he scribbled his signature a hundred times a week, and now, he struggled to put two letters together. Moving the pen close to the paper, he began to write. The letters were large and slanted like a child; his hand shook and the pen jerked across the paper.

Once finished, Greg's grip loosened and the pen dropped to the floor. A doctor took the signed form and left the couple alone. Greg looked across the room, at first at his daughter and then his wife; they did not return his gaze.

Sandra felt unable to look at the man she called her husband, the man who'd just signed away their daughter's life. Within a few minutes the doctor would come back and unplug these various machines and their daughter would be gone. Yes, it would hurt *him. Him* – that's all he was to her now; she couldn't bear to think of him as anything else apart from some man. She knew, of course, that he would be heartbroken; it was his little girl after all; she knew he loved her. She let out a sigh. Love, what did he know about love?

She had given birth!

He hadn't even been present. Some business meeting in Munich – he'd no doubt been slurping away at his coffee like he always did, trying to impress some German tyre manufacture.

Thirty six hours of labour and he couldn't make it.

He'd apologised for weeks, months even, blamed some thunderstorm for grounding the planes. At the time she accepted the apology and the flowers; however, as the years passed, the anger burned a hole in her heart. Sandra raised her head and caught his eye. She watched tears roll gently down his cheeks. She wanted to feel sorry for him, but that bastard had just convinced her to turn off her daughter's life support, and that doing so was for the best.

"We need to tell Max," said Greg.

She looked at him; there were a million things she wanted to say. Instead, she turned back to their daughter.

She rubbed her arm roughly to try and change the ever greying skin.

"San, we need to call Max."

"Phone him then, you've got a mobile, haven't you?"

"We can't use mobiles in here, the sign says —"

"It's not going to make a fat fucking load of difference now, is it? She's dead!"

They sat speechless, both unsure where Sandra's anger had originated. It was the first time she'd ever sworn at her husband.

Greg took his phone out and started to make the call.

The call was short and painful; Greg cried throughout.

A doctor came into the room; not the short, young Chinese man that had left with the consent form, but a female. She explained what she was about to do, going over the process just to make sure the couple were completely aware of the situation. Once she concluded, the hospital chaplain entered. He stood close to the bed and said a prayer. The dying girl's father moved to stand close to his wife. There was no contact. They both bowed their heads.

"Goodbye, daddy's girl. I love you forever," Greg said, choking back tears. Sandra stayed quiet.

The doctor unclipped the tube fitted to Abbie's mouth and the respiratory equipment stopped inflating.

Sandra's wailing reverberated through the hospital corridors.

MONDAY: DAY 7

FORTY-ONE

A streetlamp spilled light across the pavement; spidery shadows were cast by a nearby tree. A police car came to a halt outside Daniel Stone's house. PC Terence Bright opened the door, stepped from the car and shone a torch up the drive before getting back in and driving off.

This happened every half hour. Daniel knew because he'd been lying, fully clothed, on the bed for the last three hours, his face lit by the glow of that same streetlamp.

The old eye dressing, which had become swollen, had now been replaced by a neat gauze covering his cheek.

The curtains were open so he could see the night sky, which soothed him; it was dark but near the horizon line there were still hints of blue light.

There were many reasons he was unable to sleep.

Tonight, he felt pain in his ribs, and congealed blood rattled in his nasal passage. Two reasons that he could use, but the thing he blamed at the moment was his broken dripping shower. Once Daniel tuned into the sound it was torture, and it could only be described as what a spider would sound like if it was walking across a corrugated metal roof in clogs.

The bed creaked as he buried his head deep in a pillow, trying desperately to drown out the sound of the constantly dripping tap he'd never managed to repair. He winced at the intense pain in his ribs. In A&E a few hours earlier he'd marked it as an eight out of ten on the pain scale; as the painkillers they'd given him wore off it was still easily as bad.

He played the past week over in his head, wondering at what point he'd sunken so low. The more he tried to sleep, the more his mind raced, and if he tried to push something away it only became more prominent.

Bullet number two.

The second name.

This killing was surely going to happen; the question was when.

He knew the person well, and much like the first bullet the name was picked under duress and was a fleeting thought. Also, like the first, the second person didn't deserve to die. The sound of the patrol car slowing to a stop outside, the click of his driver's door, the twenty seconds the officer took to make sure all was well, and the thud of the door closing played out outside. Another thirty minutes without sleep had passed in what felt like seconds.

Daniel closed his eyes, but it was no good; bullet two's victim glared back at him.

He needed to warn the intended victim.

First thing in the morning he'd go to their house and explain. Then he'd call Rhodes.

A knock at the door alarmed him. The short journey downstairs and across the hallway was slow going, and his hand shook as he clutched the door handle.

"Who is it?"

"PC Bright, sir. Just wanted to inform you I'm needed back at the station. Everything seems okay out here, and we don't expect your intruder to come back. Goodnight, Mr. Stone."

Daniel heard him crunch across the gravel drive.

Five, maybe ten minutes passed. Daniel stood listening against the glass. There was nothing; still, he was scared. He returned to his room, but rather than go to bed, he took a small hold-all from the wardrobe and randomly stuffed a t-shirt, a grey hoodie, some shorts and a pair of jeans into it. He crossed the landing and took his toothbrush, toothpaste and two tins of deodorant before returning to the room and piling these in to his bag.

The second killing was inevitable; the police wouldn't be able to stop it, and then Tesar would come after him. His only option was to get away, to make sure he was nowhere near the killing so he could not be accused. There was no real thought behind his plan. He'd been planning something similar earlier, before Tesar reappeared, so now all he needed to do was find a place to go.

Another man, standing in the darkness of Daniel Stone's house, had plans of his own.

FORTY-TWO

Rain lashed against the windows of the briefing room. Rhodes listened as his colleagues complained about the weather. As outside, the atmosphere in the office was grey. There was no light-hearted banter; not even Detective Murray could muster the energy to treat them to one of his usual wisecracks. Rhodes had briefed the team with regards to Abbie Flynn's death as soon as they'd arrived.

DCI Graham entered, shook off his overcoat and took up position to one side of Rhodes.

"Go on, DI Rhodes, this is your case."

Rhodes acknowledged his superior's gesture, and could tell from Graham's face that this wasn't the first meeting he'd been to this morning. No doubt Graham's late arrival was due to having just received a rollicking from the Superintendent.

Raising his voice to be heard over the rain, he explained what needed to be done. Bottom line: Jakub Tesar must be caught that day.

"Tesar is one of the most common surnames in the Czech Republic, sir," said Bates. "And the forename is not unpopular either. I'm working on a list at present, narrowing it down from the profile Stone provided. It's almost two thousand names at present."

"Better odds than the lottery," Jackie Roberts added.

"So give me anything, the slightest hunch, anything, because I don't think this is over and we can't afford any more deaths – all our heads are on the line," said Graham.

There was nothing.

Rhodes frowned before motioning everyone to leave.

The team left, leaving Graham and Rhodes alone.

"I think we got off on the wrong foot, Patrick."

That grated. His friends called him Patrick, and Graham was not a friend.

"No, I don't think we did. You don't like me, and you're the biggest prick I've ever worked with," said Rhodes calmly.

Their eyes met, and a long pause followed before Graham spoke.

"I would remind you that I am still your *superior*!"

"Doesn't change a thing. Now, are you going to pull your head from out of the Superintendent's arse and get me some resources? You pulled PC Bright away from Stone's house last night. What if Tesar had gone back, finished the job?"

"He didn't."

"No, but there was a chance. I spoke to Bright this morning – you pulled him out to do paperwork."

"Paperwork is an important part of policing."

"Bullshit. No murderer ever got caught because someone filed their paperwork on time."

Graham got up and sauntered over to the window. He looked across the street to the school, where children and parents were starting to arrive. He rubbed his face.

"There will be no more resources. Catch him, and next time you'll have all the resources you can handle. Results, Rhodes, provide benefits."

Also standing now, Rhodes tensed, his body pressed against the table that separated him from Graham.

"I'm not a football manager being promised cash for new players if I win games. People's lives are at stake."

There was nothing more to be said; Graham's silence told Rhodes that much. Graham was out of his depth. This double murder had come too early in his CID career and, worst of all, judging from the jaded expression on his face, he'd already given up.

Rhodes left his boss and strode into the CID room.

"Joel, office please."

Murray raced in behind him.

"Shut the door and take a seat."

"What's wrong, Sir?"

"How's Katherine?"

Joel's wife was thirty-nine weeks pregnant.

"Apart from the fact she's got it in her head she wants to move, she's fine."

"Again, how long have you had the house – four, five months?"

"Six. She thinks it's too dangerous here; wants to move to Cornwall."

Rhodes smiled; Joel reminded him a lot of himself, maybe twenty years ago. Rita had wanted him to get another job and give up the force; she also said it was too dangerous.

"You told her they have crime in Cornwall, right?"

"I tried. Seems to think it's a different type of crime down there. She wants to try living in inner city Birmingham, like I did."

There was an awkward pause.

"Sir, I don't think you called me in here to talk about my life."

Rhodes stood up and looked across the office; everyone was working.

"I need you to do me a favour. Alex Burns."

"That guy I spoke to Friday? You think he has something to do with all this?"

"He lied. He was there. His wife wasn't driving his car. I know that for sure because his wife was at a book club with Rita."

Murray's gaze followed his boss's movements. He sensed his agitation.

"You want me to go and talk to him again? I take it you know his wife."

"My niece, Gemma. I want you to follow him – everywhere. He's up to something and I want him caught. I had him put away years ago; when he came out he formed a relationship with Gemma and they ended up getting married."

Murray watched as Rhodes rolled up his sleeve. "A man who does this to a police officer doesn't change his ways."

The scar looked sore; the lumps of skin around the stitching were raised and untidy. Murray had never seen the scar before, had never even heard stories about the incident. He guessed Rhodes didn't usually expose such a weakness, especially to a new colleague.

"What happened, Patrick?"

"I followed him; his gang had attacked another lad and thrown him and his bag in the canal. I knew it was him; he never denied it either. I made a mistake, I made a rash decision."

Murray noticed the anger in Rhodes's voice, but wasn't sure if he was angry with his own actions or Alex Burns.

"I followed him and some of the others into the old sugar beet site. They were spraying their usual graffiti tags and smoking weed. I cornered him, but I was taken down from behind." Rhodes rubbed the scar, as though it made the memories easier to bear.

"Burns did this with a broken bottle. I suppose I was lucky – he could have glassed my face and spoilt my good looks."

The atmosphere lightened; the officers smiled.

"Okay, Sir – he won't take a shit without you knowing."

FORTY-THREE

One of the few advantages of living in Kidderminster was its geographical location: you were never very far from the countryside.

Twelve minutes from home, Daniel shifted through the gears and accelerated out of another sharp bend and into a long straight road surrounded by fields. Worcestershire was behind him, and he was now advancing into Shropshire countryside; for once, he felt one hundred percent in control of where he was heading.

Ocean Colour Scene blasted out of the door speakers and Daniel sang along.

It had been a long night, his substitute for sleep being the energy drink and caffeine pills in his lap. What little sleep he'd managed was littered with nightmares; however, one nightmare did provide his destination. In this dream he'd seen a photo on a mantlepiece; in it was a log cabin. When he awoke, this was the only thing he remembered.

His tyres worked hard to grip the slippery tarmac as he left the town of Bridgenorth behind and headed north toward the Welsh border. An hour ahead, perhaps, and he'd be there – although he wasn't sure it still existed.

Over a decade ago, before Ollie was born, even before he and Natalie were married, they'd stumbled across a farm with chalets to rent; it was one of the greatest weekends of his life. That weekend, he realised he wanted to marry Natalie.

No sooner had they returned home than he purchased the ring. Three years later, they'd returned for their anniversary. Only two of the old chalets remained; in their place the farmer and his son were working on brand new Swedish timber log cabins. The plans were magnificent. Each one would have a decked area with hot tubs – their unique selling point, according to the farmer. Hot tubs held no appeal for Daniel. It was something about taking a bath outdoors with other people; he just didn't understand it.

Natalie and Daniel always planned to return, but that was before the split.

Daniel hoped the farmer still owned the land. Taking another swig from his energy drink, Daniel cruised; the further he drove the more relaxed he felt. He crossed into Wales and a weight lifted. The more miles that ticked over, the more victim two's image faded.

He'd entered another country. There was no way the police could pin anything on him this time.

The petrol gauge showed the tank was almost empty; in his urgency to leave, this small fact had slipped his mind. The price at the first petrol station was a little higher than back home – less competition out here in the small towns of mid-Wales. He filled the tank and almost bounced into the shop he felt so good. Browsing, he picked up a pack of chewing gum, two cans of lager and a Pot Noodle. A few quick supplies, nothing too fancy; just enough to tide him over. Once he got to the lodge he'd drive out for more – no point stocking up only to find the farm and cabins no longer existed.

"Number one, please," Daniel told the cashier. He was a young lad, eighteen, maybe nineteen, and wore baggy jeans which hung over steel toe-capped boots, and a green knitted sweater. His nose had a silver stud in and his lip a ring. He scanned the items and shot Daniel a look of disdain.

Daniel put the rudeness down to his age. In his happy mood, Daniel had forgotten his less than tidy appearance, which might have caused the boy to stare. After all, before him stood a thirtyfive-year-old with a bandage on his right hand, a dressing across his eye, evidence of a recently broken nose and a yellow, swollen cheek.

"Fifty four pounds," the lad said with a grunt.

Daniel paid and left. He ran across the concrete and ducked into his car to avoid a sudden downpour.

FORTY-FOUR

Six times they'd played the video footage; three times at full speed, a couple in slow motion and the last, one a frame at a time.

Rhodes's computer let out a wild buzz as the fan kicked in.

His coffee sat cold and untouched.

Rhodes knew there was something missing.

Viewing number seven showed an empty station. The train, which both Abbie Flynn and Daniel Stone had boarded a week ago, slowed as it entered Kidderminster station. Rhodes watched Abbie Flynn leave the third carriage from the front and walk briskly up the ramp.

He paused the recording.

He zoomed in on her face. She looked happy; definitely no sign of fear. Her boyfriend Toby had said in his statement that her parents were not aware she was coming home. She had wanted to surprise them, and maybe that was the excitement she appeared to have on her face. It was odd to see her like that, oblivious to what would follow.

Now he zoomed in on Stone, who came from the same exit four seconds later. Stone looked the same: no real malice or anger present. In fact, he wasn't even looking at the girl ahead of him, but struggling with the inside pocket of his suit jacket.

The video loop began again; Rhodes concentrated on Stone, recalling his statement. Halfway up the exit ramp, Stone was still fumbling in his pocket; Rhodes hit pause again. Stone retrieved a phone and nothing else from the pocket. Rhodes focused on the screen, his chin resting on clenched hands, his elbows planted on the edge of the desk. He reached across and took a sip from his coffee, spitting it back into the cup.

A copy of Stone's statement lay open on the desk and Rhodes re-examined it. Stone claimed that he'd dropped his phone, and while searching for it a group of youths had attacked him. The only bit of this story that played out on the recording was the dropping of the phone. Maybe the beating occurred on the street, but his lack of injuries on the tape threw this account into doubt.

There was a knock and Jackie Roberts entered, carrying a fresh coffee.

"Thought you could do with a top-up."

Rhodes smiled – she'd practically read his mind. He gestured at her to join him. "Thanks," she said, and sat down.

"What am I missing, Jackie?"

"You want my honest opinion, Sir?"

"Always." He took a sip – it was good coffee.

"Nothing, you are missing nothing — there's Abbie Flynn's killer." She pointed to Daniel Stone.

"You have a theory?"

"What's Stone really like? You questioned him. So what kind of a person is he?"

"He's not a bad man. I didn't like him when I originally went to the hospital. I've seen him since – he seems okay. Devoted father, by all accounts a friendly neighbour, and according to Bates even his ex-wife was full of praise."

"Do you think he attacked Miss Flynn?"

"I don't know. I do know that when I broke down his door he was extremely fearful; whatever Stone's capable of, Tesar is capable of a whole lot more."

"I don't know, Patrick, maybe he didn't mean to do it, maybe he was at a low point and this attack was fuelled by alcohol and ill-feeling – it just happened."

Rhodes sat back in his chair.

"If this wasn't premeditated, then how is it linked to Rogers' killing?"

"The way I see it, we're looking at the wrong person for the connection."

"So what connection are we looking for?"

"We need to see how Jakub Tesar is connected to Abbie Flynn. My theory: we find that connection, we'll solve this. University towns are full of all types of people."

"What, like middle-aged Czech salesmen?"

Jackie flicked her hair out of her eyes. She seemed to glow in the soft daylight coming through the office blinds. Rhodes found it near impossible not to just stare at her.

"Sounds unlikely, but, like DCI Graham said, how many of us really told our parents who we were sleeping with at that age? There's a possibility Abbie found herself an older man and that man is now taking his revenge on Daniel Stone."

"If he wanted revenge and he killed Rogers, why didn't he just kill Stone when he had the chance?"

"Because he enjoys the hunt?"

A knock interrupted the conversation. Bates stood in the open doorway.

"Crooks is heading over to Templeton's place again. He just got a call from one of the owners; Templeton's van has just been broken into."

"Isn't that a job for uniform?"

"Seems Crooks made himself a new friend and she phoned him direct. The man who broke in is still inside."

"Okay. Let me know if there are any developments."

Rhodes ran the tape again. Nothing changed, nothing at all. Abbie still got off the train. Stone still got off the train. Abbie Flynn still made it off the platform. Stone still rummaged for his phone. That was it. All was still as it had been one week ago.

"There are too many weirdos connected to this; that Templeton guy is up to no good. We have Tesar, Stone, and I'm not ruling Burns out."

Roberts brushed her fringe out of her eyes and gave Rhodes a look of disapproval.

"What?"

"He may have been in the area at the time, but God, Patrick, it seems a bit desperate to try to pin this on him. We all know the history, but I think you need to start thinking that maybe, just maybe, he's changed."

Rhodes liked Roberts, and he valued her opinion. This time, however, she was wrong and Rhodes knew it; he just had to wait for Alex Burns to make a mistake and he would be there to put him where he belonged.

FORTY-FIVE

The queue at the counter was two deep. Tammy Cavendish was dressed in a tiny vest that showed more of her cleavage that was normally deemed acceptable this early in the morning. She also had on a pair of leggings that looked like she'd need to cut them to get them off. She tapped away on her phone as she waited for the man in front of her, who smelt like he hadn't washed for a week, to pay for his two-litre bottle of strong cider and five cans of cat food.

She didn't hear the crying to start with; it didn't register. But people had started to point and whisper.

She looked around and saw a face she recognised. She didn't know the lady well, but she'd seen her around town. She mostly detested her. The woman drove around in her Mercedes like she owned the place, with perfect make-up and impeccably styled hair.

Sandra Flynn looked the polar opposite today. She was dressed in jogging trousers three sizes too big, a baggy hoodie and no make-up. Her hair was scraped back, she looked awful, and she was crying – in fact, sobbing.

Bubbles of snot formed and popped, and spit dribbled down her lips.

Sandra was at the money changing kiosk; two members of staff were trying to talk to her, but to no effect. Her pleas got louder.

"Please take it back – my daughter died last night, we can't go on holiday now. Please!" She was largely incoherent, but Tammy picked up the gist of what she said.

It made her feel sick. Abbie Flynn was her age. She had been attacked on Monday night. Two days later Tammy had been followed by a taxi in Worcester. She moved along to the till and paid for her shopping, but before she left she took another glance at Sandra Flynn. She now lay in a heap on the floor, a security guard trying his best to calm her.

Tammy looked at her phone and pressed play on a video clip. She couldn't watch it again; she knew what it showed. But as she walked away from the store, a young girl's screams could be heard from the speaker on her handset.

FORTY-SIX

Colin Templeton swiped his card across the sensor and waited for the barrier to rise before driving forward at the stated 'five mile per hour' speed limit.

He passed the field that curved around in front of the site's clubhouse. At the end of the field he pulled left and parked the car in the small space allocated to his caravan. He grabbed his lunch bag from the passenger seat and plodded to the door.

It was unlocked. It was always unlocked, for two reasons. Firstly, he felt safe around here; secondly, he didn't believe he owned anything worth stealing.

The room was dark – the sun always hit the back of the van at this time of day, what little sun there was. His plot was one of the worst on the park for sunlight, hidden under a row of overgrown horse chestnut trees. When it rained, like today, it felt like night inside.

Colin refrained from switching on any lights, a habit he'd slipped into when his mother was still alive. Switching lights on would have woken her.

He made his way in darkness along the thin hallway to the bigger of the two box bedrooms, the one where his mother had spent her final years. He pulled a towel from the wardrobe and undressed, leaving his clothes in a pile on the floor. He made his way back to the living area.

Colin loved the freedom the death of his mother had given him; he dropped the towel by the door for the shower. He didn't care if anyone could see him; this was his home and his body.

If he had put the towel on he would have dropped it as he re-entered the front room. There was a man sitting on the sofa in front of him, his face a mere outline in the shadows.

"What the fucking hell are you doing?"

The man stood up. "Shut up and sit there," he said, pointing to the sofa.

Colin tried to grab something to cover himself up; the only thing in reach was a stained tea towel on the work surface.

"I suggest you get out, now!" Colin raised his voice at the end of his sentence in an attempt to hide his fear.

"Stand then, arsehole! Good idea, actually – get some use out of your legs while you still can."

"What do you want?"

Alex Burns emerged from the shadows, a smile plastered across his face. He held an ornament in his hand, a figurine of a ballet dancer in blue and white pastel. The dancer's expression was full of concentration.

"You remember me, Colin?"

Colin backed away. "No."

Burns advanced so that he was inches away from Colin, who was pinned against the kitchen surface.

Fragments of porcelain shot through the air, the figurine crushed in Alex Burns's hand. Colin felt Alex's breath on his face, warm and smelling of mint chewing

GAVIN JONES

gum. He tensed as Burns gripped his testicles and started to squeeze. He felt too the dust of the ballet dancer settle on his skin.

"Come on Colin, you have to remember *me*?"

Colin knew exactly who he was, and, more to the point, what he was capable of.

"Yes, I remember – I saw you at the pub the other day."

The pressure on Colin's testicles intensified. Colin gulped; liquid formed in the back of his throat, the sort that is usually followed by vomit.

"Don't tell me you've forgotten how you stitched me up before – got me sacked for stealing because you took a dislike to me. If we don't know each other, how the hell did I know where to find you, mommy's boy?"

The last two words chilled Colin more than anything. 'Mommy's boy' was what the guys at the taxi firm used to call him. It was also the last thing Alex Burns had said to him a few years back: *you'll pay for this, mummy's boy!*

Colin tried to convince Alex he was clueless. He panted hard as his testicles were freed. "Let me put some clothes on and we can straighten this out," he said.

"No, I don't think so. You see, I never forgot about how you did that. It was so easy for them to think it was me – I did have a criminal record."

"Come on, give me a break."

Alex did just that; in fact, he gave him two breaks, both through the right humerus. He moved quickly, pushing Colin against the fake marble kitchen surface and smashing his arm across the oven top.

Colin yelped as he hit the floor, but he wasn't there long. Alex dragged him to his feet, holding him an inch or so off the floor so that their eyes were level.

Colin took a deep breath; from Alex's expression the attack was far from over. He took his punishment, staying silent as he was punched this way and that.

"It was the girl from the pub, not me!" Colin forced the words through blood-spattered teeth as the beating stopped for a second.

FORTY-SEVEN

Tori Vilani raced across the grass toward the caravan, leapt up the two steps and swung the caravan door open, "Police!" she announced, half expecting the attacker to still be there.

She entered in a quick seamless move. In front of her lay a naked, unconscious Colin Templeton. DC Steven Crooks came in behind his colleague and stood feet from a near-lifeless Templeton.

"I'll call for an ambulance."

Colin squinted up at them. "He's gone after the girl."

"What girl?"

"From the pub, opposite the station in Kidderminster."

"Who has?"

Colin struggled to breathe. Even though he was in pain, he grinned as he spoke. "Alex Burns – he did this, and I think the girl is next."

FORTY-EIGHT

Electrically-controlled black iron railings framed the hundred-year-old mansion. Rhodes had seen gates like this before, and there were usually fierce-looking dogs patrolling beyond them. Security like this meant one of two things: to keep people out, or to keep them in.

He pressed a buzzer and announced his intentions to a lady on the other end. She sounded pleasant. The gates opened slowly; their sheer weight meant it was impossible for them to move any faster.

He parked his car on a pristine white shingle driveway, each stone of which looked as though it had been washed several times before being placed there with measured symmetry.

A lady stood waiting in a wooden, church-like door frame, which led to a bright porch. "Detective Inspector Rhodes, do come in."

Natalie Gibbs had a stunning smile; the product of extensive dental work no doubt, Rhodes thought. He knew she was in her early thirties, but she looked younger. Her hair hung loose and gleamed, even in the grey light of the dull day. She wore black jeans and a baggy lemon-coloured t-shirt with a gold and diamond cross motif emblazed across it.

"Thank you," Rhodes said, following her down a wide hallway.

He tried hard not to look nosy, but he needed to see as much of the house as he could. It was amazing. A marble floor led to an ivory staircase, which curved away towards an upper balcony.

"My husband shouldn't be long – training finished an hour ago."

"It's actually you I came to see, Mrs. Gibbs."

They entered the lounge, the carpet almost engulfing Rhodes's shoes, and took a seat.

"Me? I thought you'd come about the racist tweets Tom's been getting. Is he okay?" She looked shocked.

"As far as I'm aware. I'm here to ask you a few questions about your husband; sorry – ex-husband."

"Dan."

Oddly, there was warmth in her tone; not at all what he'd been expecting. Experience taught him that if you mentioned an ex to most divorcées, you could see their resentment manifest itself in their physical behaviour. Natalie was the complete opposite; even DC Bates's report didn't indicate this much affection.

"Are you aware that he may have been attacked last week?"

"Yeah; we dropped Ollie off to the hospital to see him, then one of your team came to ask few questions. Daniel didn't look too bad. Is he okay?"

"Do you have regular contact with him?"

"Not really. Ollie sees him weekends, but unless there are any problems with Ollie or we need to swap weekends, then, no – we don't speak."

"Not the best of splits, then?"

"I don't see what this has got to do with him getting attacked."

"We're trying to paint a picture, Mrs. Gibbs, of the kind of person Daniel is, and I just needed some background. We don't have any information on his parents, say, so you're the next best thing. Obviously, with him being your ex-husband, your character reference could be somewhat negative."

"Actually, Inspector, Daniel is a fantastic man, and a great dad – a kind and loving man. Sometimes he was too nice."

"So he never raised a hand to you, or anything like that?"

"God, no. Daniel and I hit a bad patch; we were having problems before we had Ollie."

"So having Ollie made it worse?"

"Having Ollie didn't repair the cracks. Our attention turned to him and we forgot the problems for a while, but the cracks widened and finally, from my point of view anyway, they became too wide to pull back together, so I left."

"How did it affect Daniel?"

"He was distraught, but I think it was Ollie he missed, not me."

"Did he get angry, then?"

"No, he cried a lot on the phone, and I listened; that was the least I could do. I'd been having an affair, which I've never admitted to him. Tom and I moved in nine months later, but we'd been together about three months prior to the split. At one point I thought Daniel knew. He caught me on the phone and we argued about it. I denied everything. He either believed me or knew I was lying and didn't want to admit it to himself, and we just moved on."

"What about suicide? Would losing his job have been the final straw?"

Natalie looked hard at Detective Rhodes, a little surprised.

"I didn't know he'd lost his job. I don't think it would make a difference though. I don't want this to sound nasty, but I don't think he'd have the balls. I've seen him depressed. When his brother died, he went into his shell and we hardly spoke for a year; I should have gotten out then, but he was so vulnerable."

"A brother – there's no mention in his file of a brother."

"Yeah – Jake. He was nine years older."

"Jake Stone. I'll have to check that out."

"I would check for Jake Carpenter."

"Carpenter - different dads?"

"No, Daniel changed his name to his mother's maiden name the day he turned sixteen. His father was a violent man. Daniel was always too young to stand up for himself, but Jake wasn't – when he was eighteen he left and joined the army. Daniel's father died six months later."

"Did Jake and Daniel get on?"

Through the window Rhodes could see that the rain had started again. Out on the lawn a man tended to the flowerbeds. Somewhere within the house, there was a smell of meat cooking. It smelt good. Rhodes took the house in again. He understood why Natalie Gibbs had gotten out of her relationship with Daniel Stone.

"Yeah – it was strange, really. The age difference didn't seem to matter."

"How did Jake die?"

There was a pause as Natalie composed herself. It was all still raw.

"We booked a holiday cottage in Yorkshire, and Jake came along and brought his girlfriend. We were out having a meal; the boys stayed on for another drink while we went home. They were walking home when a group of youths confronted them. Daniel would have been petrified, but not Jake; he stood up for himself. Three of them started laying into him. Daniel tried to do something but they knocked him to the ground and stamped on his head. Jake managed to break one lad's arm and another's nose, then they ran off. He was helping Daniel when one of the youths came back and smashed a metal bar over his head; two days later he died from his injuries. All I remember is running from the cottage toward the railway station and seeing the flashing lights. They were just lying in pools of blood. Daniel changed, and I hated the person it turned him into. Ollie came along and, well, he returned to the way he'd always been."

Rhodes stopped asking questions. Something more important was now going through his head. What was the chance of lightning striking twice? The story was a smokescreen. Daniel had invented the Tesar figure to send the police down a dead-end. This didn't explain the attack at the house; Rhodes had seen the injuries. He needed to make a call. He needed a medical opinion.

"Do you think Daniel had any enemies?"

"Not at all. He wasn't that sort of man, he didn't make enemies."

"Any links to the Czech Republic?"

"Um, Jake might have served there for a couple of months, back in the early nineties I think. It might have been Yugoslavia. I get all those places mixed up."

Rhodes thanked Natalie for her time and left the house, making a call on the way to the car. He phoned the force medical contact Dr. Suzanne Clough. He asked her a few questions relating to head injuries, got some answers, thanked her for her time and disconnected.

A red light blinked on his Blackberry. Joel Murray had left him a message: Call me ASAP. Rhodes rang his DS straight away. As he listened to Joel Murray's report, he smiled.

Rhodes finished the call and took a long look at himself in the rear view mirror. "Now I'm going to get you – that's for sure!"

He went to pull away, but a young boy stood in front of his car. He buzzed down his window. The boy looked nervous. He was staring at the ground, his hair dripping with rainwater.

"You okay, son?"

He looked up. It was then that Rhodes recognised him – a younger version of Daniel Stone.

"Are you the police?" the boy asked.

Rhodes couldn't understand how he knew this but answered anyway, "Yes, I'm a police officer. Why don't you go inside? You'll catch a cold out here."

"I'm okay. I'm always okay."

Rhodes believed it, and believed he always would be. It was trait that must have been passed on from father to son. Daniel Stone had been thrown a lot of bad luck over the years, but the deeper Rhodes dug down, the stronger the man seemed.

The boy leaned closer to the open window, looking beyond the detective and staring at the inside of the car.

"If you're the police, why aren't you wearing a uniform?"

"I'm a detective – we wear our own clothes."

Rhodes thought that was the end of the conversation. He could see the boy thinking about walking away, but at the last second he seemed to change his mind.

"I'm going to be a detective when I'm bigger. Do you have a gun?"

"No, sorry, no gun."

Ollie's disappointment showed. "Oh. Can you help my dad, please?" His words were quiet and clear.

"Does he need our help?"

"I think so," the lad replied. His nervousness increased; he struggled to keep still.

"Come on, mate – you need to tell me more, otherwise I won't be able to help and that's what we do. Let's start with a name."

There another long pause.

"His name is Daniel Stone, and I think someone is after him."

"After him? What do you mean? Has your father gotten himself into some trouble?"

"Not sure…someone is trying to kill him, I think."

"I don't think that's very likely."

There was anger in the child's eyes.

"My mate's sister probably thought that and she's dead now."

Rhodes didn't answer. He sensed the boy's fear.

"He was really strange at the weekend and he was trying to be all fun like he normally is, but I think he's really scared of something."

"I tell you what – I'm on my way back to the station now; I'll check it out."

"Thanks, Mister. I'm definitely going to be a policeman when I'm older."

"That's good – we need all the good men we can get."

"Or, a Formula 1 driver."

They both smiled.

The innocence of youth was something Rhodes still cherished; even the hardships of his job hadn't robbed him of that.

The boy turned, gave a wave, and trudged toward his house.

The gates opened.

Rhodes buzzed up the window, his trousers drenched from the rain. He had a criminal to catch, and doing so would make him very happy.

FORTY-NINE

The rain that lashed the window of the pub was loud and constant. Tammy was alone behind the bar. The rain was heavy but hadn't forced any of the usual rats scurrying in for cover.

She stared down at the bright screen of her phone. A video played over and over. The colour had left her face, her eyes were puffy from lack of sleep and her hair was a mess.

The doors clicked open and she raised her eyes from her phone. In front of her stood the exact same face her phone had been playing for the past hour: Alex Burns. His body filled the doorway; he looked bigger than he had done last time she had seen him, crumpled in agony on his living room floor. He didn't look so weak now. He looked angry.

"What do you think you're doing in here?" she asked.

He took a step closer and spoke softly. "I need a word with your father."

"He's not here."

Under the cover of the bar, she scrolled out of her videos and locked her phone.

Alex took two more steps forward.

His look sent a shiver down her spine. She prepared for what she knew was coming.

"Good!" Alex said through gritted teeth.

He bounded forward, clutched her hair and dragged her over the counter in one movement. Drip trays and beer mats fell to the floor and two bar stools toppled with a crash.

"Tell me what you saw!"

Tammy's scalp felt like it been prised from her head. She couldn't believe this was happening. Her father would be so disappointed in her. She was disappointed in herself. She had let her guard down and this would get her father into trouble again. He wouldn't let something like this go unpunished.

Their lives had changed so much since her father had gotten out of his old life in Liverpool. She hadn't known what he did then. All she knew was that he would come home late at night, sometimes with a broken nose or a cut lip. Every night, bloody or not, he would give her a kiss, thinking she was asleep; she never was, not until she finally heard him get into bed. She only ever felt safe when he was around. He was not around now. She tried to put on a brave face.

"No!" she yelled in Alex's face.

This angered him even more and he flung her on to a sofa by the pool table. He stood back and looked down at her.

"Not so cocky now, are you? What is it you want, you stupid little girl? Money?"

Tammy let out a laugh. It hurt to laugh, but she was determined not to cry.

"So you have yourself a crush, and you have a neat little way of blackmailing me."

"A crush – are you joking? I don't need to blackmail you to get you in bed."

"You have nothing to tell – there was nothing to see!"

She knew he didn't believe this; he knew what had happened. He didn't know what, if any part, she'd been witness to and that fact was cutting him up inside.

"So, why are you here? You're making out I'm some sort of scheming slut."

"I wouldn't say you were a slut, but you have been banged more times than a snooze button on a Monday morning."

There was a smile from Tammy. "How original – did you get that off one of your friends' Facebook statuses? Oh, I forgot – you'd need actual friends for that, though, wouldn't you?"

He slapped her hard across the face and she whimpered in pain. She had never felt such intense pain in her life. She felt like she was going to be sick. Her father had taught her to defend herself, but not how to deal with the pain if she couldn't.

"Hurts, don't it?"

Vilely twisted, his face repulsed her. The corners of his mouth foamed like a rabid dog. An animal; that was all she could think he was. She looked deep into his eyes. He wasn't in the room with her; his stare seemed to say he was somewhere else, as though his mind had switched off so he didn't register what he was doing now.

She tried hard to come up with a plan. She knew that if she didn't stop him he would kill her. She was no real match for him; she had been lucky the other day.

Alex pulled his hand back to slap her again. His hand never made the full swing; instead, he felt a force behind him pushing him forward. The next thing he saw was the edge of the pool table as his head smashed against it. He crumpled to the floor.

Mark Cavendish stood above him, his face contorted with anger, his coat dripping with rainwater. He glanced at his daughter, who gave him a nod.

He smiled. A smile that said, don't worry Tammy, Daddy's going to sort this out. Her father took a pool cue from the table, and used the heavy end to hammer blows down on Alex.

"You an idiot, boy? You come into my pub to pick a fight, you certainly don't pick it with my daughter. If you tried with me, maybe I would have given you enough respect to walk away. But lay a hand on her? *Dumb* is not the word."

He lifted the pool cue high above his head, but as he brought it back down it was snatched out of his hand.

"I'm going to have to stop you right there."

Rhodes snapped the cue in half and discarded the pieces.

"That's my property you just broke!"

"Looks like you broke something of mine, so we're quits."

Rhodes looked down at Alex Burns's unconscious body while keeping one eye on Cavendish, only yards away, just in case he tried anything.

"No, I don't think we are."

"Ok, send me the bill."

Noise from outside entered the pub as the cavalry arrived. Murray looked a little shocked that Rhodes was in there. Vilani and Crooks had worked with the DI a little longer so expected him.

Seeing more police in his pub infuriated Mark Cavendish.

Then the atmosphere took an even darker turn as the landlord lashed out at Rhodes. Rhodes expected it and ducked; the fist missed his left ear by half an inch. An inch closer than he'd anticipated.

Cavendish was fast, and threw a right.

Rhodes leaned backwards and caught the fist in the palm of his hand. It hurt. There was a lot of power in the man's punch.

The other police officers waded in and tackled Cavendish to the floor; Vilani dealt with Tammy, who, even though she was clearly in severe pain, tried hard to vent her aggression on the female detective.

"I thought I told you to stay out of my pub!" Cavendish yelled as he struggled on the floor.

Rhodes just stepped past him. "You did. I took no notice."

"I deal with the problems in here," Cavendish said, now back on his feet, handcuffed and being restrained by Murray and Crooks.

Rhodes was pleased that a pulse still ran through Burns's veins, and even more pleased that he'd soon be able to snap some cuffs on him.

He took a look a Tammy, then at her father. He sympathised a little. If someone had laid a finger on his daughter, he'd have wanted to do the exact same thing.

"If you carry on dealing with things yourself, then I become your problem and I promise you one thing, you don't want that."

"Don't I? Are you sure about that? You're a small-town cop – I've dealt with more criminals than your entire force."

"Thanks for the help. We owe you one."

As they led the landlord out to a police van, he gave a parting shot.

"One day, Rhodes, you're going to regret this."

Rhodes, who was three or four paces behind, brushed himself down. "I don't think I will."

A second van arrived and two uniformed officers jumped out. Rhodes pointed to where Burns lay and explained that the paramedics were on their way. He told them to allow the medics to do their bit, but under no circumstances should they be allowed to take Burns to hospital. It would be a hard task convincing them, but Rhodes wanted Burns in for questioning that afternoon.

FIFTY

The book he was reading reminded him of the book all the women in the office had not stopped talking about last year, for months gushing - *Fifty Shades* this, *Fifty Shades* that. He decided then that it wasn't for him. Whips and bondage didn't appeal, so the hysteria had passed him by.

And so the green of the surrounding landscape replaced the grey of the title. An amazing panorama: fields, trees, mountains. He had forgotten the sheer magnificence of the landscape here. Unlike most of the memories he'd held dear, this hadn't been spoilt by the passage of time; a few new buildings had sprung up in the distance, but they hadn't marred the view.

He rested his arms between the barbs of the wire fence that marked the boundaries between the path and a field of sheep. Time stood still for no-one, but memories could rewind the clock. Daniel rewound to a decade ago as he gazed blissfully out into that landscape. He felt younger, his body thinner, his hair a little thicker, his life simpler. He recalled a time when everything was easier, when he was with the woman he loved; when he was happy. He had felt then that life would play out like that forever.

"Hello there."

Daniel turned to see the owner of the farm behind him. His trousers and shirt were covered in mud and oil.

"Maggie says you want a lodge for a couple of nights. She said to put you in Redwing; that's the third one along."

Daniel followed the line of the farmer's finger down the slight hill to the third plot along and the wooden lodge: square-shaped, dark wood finish, a large area of decking out front, with a plastic table and chairs. The decking was mostly taken up by a hot tub.

The farmer came a little closer. "She said you wanted to pay cash. I don't know if you noticed, but Maggie says a lot."

"If that's okay. Did Maggie say that would be okay?"

Both men smiled.

"Sure, as long as you're not on the run from the police."

There was a moment of silence as the two men stared at each other. Then the farmer started to chuckle.

"I'm just trying to recuperate," said Daniel. "Letting these injuries heal."

"I'm joking," said the farmer.

"I know I look a bit weird – I had an accident."

"Don't worry, I've seen worse – seen a man try to dislodge an object blocking the blades of a combine harvester... What happened there makes your wounds look like a pinprick, my lad."

Again the farmer laughed. Daniel did not. He was in a rush now. He wanted the keys and he wanted to get inside away from everyone.

If he'd known the exact reason Daniel was hiding out, maybe he wouldn't have been so quick to smile, Daniel thought, taking the keys.

He made his way to the lodge. The inside was perfect. Dark walls and ceilings, modern leather sofa, scatter cushions, a plasma TV hanging above a log burner. The kitchen took up one side of the building and the first bedroom the other side. There were two single beds, a wardrobe and a small dressing table. Two doors led from the corridor. The smaller one on the right led to a slate-tiled shower room. He tested the shower: powerful, more powerful than the one at home. There was a fresh scent of lavender throughout.

Daniel switched off the light and entered the room on the left. The master bedroom was magnificent. Most of it was taken up by a double bed. He dropped his backpack and took out his laptop. The signal from the WiFi was not strong, but it worked. He could see trees through his window, and the sky beyond. It was a brilliant blue. He relaxed fully and started typing the name Jakub Tesar. He tried the the obvious places first, Google and social networking sites, before moving onto dating websites and newspaper archives. Daniel found no one who matched his tormenter's description. The minutes drifted by. He tried to find an image of the gun. That was simpler; it did not take long. All he had to do was to find a connection between the man and the gun.

When he looked over he had two missed calls from Ollie.

He called him back and they spoke for about twenty minutes. Ollie informed him a policeman had come to speak to his Mom. From the description, Daniel worked out that it had been Patrick Rhodes. Ollie then went in to great detail about the night he had planned. An evening of football; Manchester United were playing Tottenham. Tom Gibbs had bought a new 3D TV for their cinema room and tonight Ollie was allowed have four friends around to watch the match.

He didn't mind his son's excitement. He couldn't blame him; he was only twelve.

Ollie then said that his mom was going out for the night with some old friends. Daniel recognised their names. He had been friends with them too, before the split. Most were divorced and had remarried. Daniel played a game with Ollie, guessing where they were going. Ollie had to ask his mother, but grudgingly confirmed that his father was right: an old wine bar, far from the limelight and prying paparazzi she had now become accustomed to.

Daniel told his son he loved him. You too, Ollie said. There was a click on the line and Daniel was sure he heard another man's voice before he went silent.

FIFTY-ONE

Rhodes smiled as he leaned back in his chair. Next to him in interview room three was DC Tori Vilani. Across from them was Alex Burns, his face battered, his hair matted with clumps of dry blood. Next to him was Simon Ainsworth, a smartly-dressed, fair-haired, pale young man who looked entirely out of his depth.

Ainsworth paid more attention to the camera in the corner of the room than what was being said - which, so far, hadn't been much. Rhodes was trying hard to antagonise Burns, who was seconds from biting.

"Wife goes away and you revert to type, right? I think we're all aware of what a hard man you think you are. A broken arm – what did your friend Colin do to deserve that; and that sweet girl from the pub, seems you upset her as well. You fancy elaborating?"

There was no answer.

"Come on Alex, there has to be a reason. We've checked the records. You worked together four years ago. Was it something from back then that's been simmering?" Vilani asked.

Still no answer.

"Okay, I've had enough of this, Alex," said Rhodes. "Let me tell you something about Colin Templeton, shall I? I've had the misfortune of meeting him myself only once before – last week in fact. Horrible little man. Personally, I don't blame you for hitting him – I fancied doing it myself."

Rhodes paused for a second, giving Alex just enough time to reply, but jumping in and stopping him as his lips opened.

"Do you want to know whose name got mentioned in that conversation we had?"

"Mine."

"Got it in one: you. He gave me a bit of information, which you later denied. Now I know for sure you're lying, so do you want to hear my theory?"

"No."

"Well, you're going to anyway. You were asked a simple question; let's see if you can remember the answer. Were you driving past the train station at approximately ten o'clock on Monday the 22nd of April?"

Rhodes waited for a reply; none came.

"You're a Wolves fan, right?"

Still no reply.

"Come on Alex, staying quiet is going to get you nowhere – just answer some of DI Rhodes's questions," Vilani added.

Alex leaned forward with a sigh. "Think you'll find they're more statements than questions. I'll tell you exactly what happened on Monday night and then you can let me go. I went to the cricket club to watch the Wolves, I had a few drinks, then walked home. Before you ask: no, I didn't pass the station. I went down Chester Road and up the alleyway by the car sales place and then over the footbridge, back past the Harriers. I'll close the door on my way out, shall I?"

"Walked. How long did that take you?"

"Not sure – fifteen minutes?"

"So what time did you get back?"

"Just past ten. *News at Ten* was just starting."

"They played Crystal Palace, didn't they?"

"Charlton."

"That's it – I knew it was some London club. Saw the result in the paper. You must have been happy with Wolves scoring in the seventh minute of injury time then?"

"What are we doing, Patrick, having a friendly football conversation? Yeah, I was delighted with the late goal. You're wasting my time. Let's chat about Saturday afternoon instead."

"We can talk about Saturday after we talk about today, but first, I'm more interested in last Monday night. I need some help with a little theory I have."

Rhodes got up.

"I'm not a big football fan, so do correct me if any of this is wrong. Kick-off was at eight o'clock. Forty-five minutes, maybe a few minutes for injuries. Takes us to quarter to nine; then fifteen for the break, another forty-five for the second half. Okay, I make that nine forty-five. Add to that your fifteen-minute walk and we get you arriving home at ten, just like you said."

"Yeah, exactly like I said."

"Only, that's the bit I'm struggling with. You just said Wolves scored in the ninety-seventh minute and you stayed to watch it all, so nine forty-five, add seven, plus the time for you to leave. Anyone else feel like we're on *Countdown*? Leaves you eight minutes to walk home. Eight minutes from the cricket club to your house isn't too long by car, but not if you have to make a stop at the station first. You ready to start telling us the truth?"

"No comment."

The room went quiet.

"You're in a massive pile of shit, Alex, and you know it. You want to know how I know? You've lost your 'big man' attitude. That tiny brain of yours is ticking over double-time just trying to think of a way out."

"Don't need one – you've no proof that any of what you just said happened. So sit down, old man, before you really make a fool of yourself!"

"I'll sit down once I've seen you sent down."

The detectives tried for another hour to get some sort of sense out of Alex Burns, but he'd clammed up. Just repeated 'no comment' throughout. They showed him some photos of Templeton – he was unmoved. They showed him some photos of Tammy Cavendish, he was unmoved. Then Rhodes slipped a rogue photo in the pile.

A photo of Abbie Flynn.

Rhodes noticed something behind his pretence at being unmoved by that one – something spooked him for a second when he first laid eyes on the dead girl's face.

FIFTY-TWO

The smell of chlorine drifted through the crisp night air; there was a faint hum of electricity and the flutter of bubbles popping. Multicoloured LED lights lit up the hot tub like a UFO.

As first experiences go, this was pretty pleasant. The warmth of the water was in perfect contrast to the breeze on his clammy face.

There was no one-else out there; no lights in the other seven unoccupied cabins.

He felt for his watch, which sat precariously on the rim of the moulded-plastic frame. It was 11:33pm – another quarter of an hour and he would retreat to his temporary wooden home and sleep. A long, pleasant night of sleep was just what he needed.

The combination of fresh mountain air, the warmth of the tub and the small amount alcohol he'd consumed made an ideal alternative to the prescription sleeping pills he'd received whilst in A&E.

The sporadic bleating of nearby sheep and the odd lonesome toot of an owl were the only sounds to break the silence. In the distance, a white ball of light moved quickly along winding country lanes.

Daniel kept his eyes on that light. Someone was in a desperate rush. He tried to guess who, like it was a game. He sometimes did this when in a café or restaurant. He'd pick one person and watch them for a while, making up a story in his head about their life.

In the car, he supposed now, was a local youth who knew the roads like the back of his hand. Maybe he was showing off for a girl.

No, it was a doctor on call, trying to reach an ailing patient.

Or a vet – there was a sick cow and the poor driver had only a few minutes before he would be elbow deep in arsehole.

Daniel was snapped out of his thoughts by a voice.

"Bit late for that, isn't it?"

Half ready to either jump out or submerge himself, Daniel tried to pin-point the person's location in the darkness.

"Hi… Just wanted to try it," Daniel fumbled.

The man got closer and rested his arms on the decking rail. He steadied himself; Daniel could see he'd found it hard to walk along the dark path toward the lodge. Even from twenty or so yards away, Daniel realised that the farmer was drunk.

"Never been in one myself. Maggie says they're relaxing. I think it's like having a bath outside. Sometimes I see five or six people in them. Could you imagine that, having a bath with your whole family, and outside too?"

"First time for me too. It says not to spend too long in them, in your welcome manual."

"Maggie says the manuals need updating. Everything needs updating. I wish I could go back to farming, but needs must and all that, eh, *manure*. Maggie says I drink too much. Do you think I drink too much?"

"I don't even know you, so couldn't possibly pass comment."

"I like you. Maggie said you looked strange, but I knew you were a nice guy first time I saw you."

"I was watching that car out there in the hills. He was going fast – what's out there?"

"I didn't see a car, sorry. Probably some drunken farmer driving home from the pub."

With that the farmer stumbled away up the drive.

Now that he had been interrupted, Daniel decided to call it a night. He could feel the skin on his fingers had ridged from time spent in the water.

He dried himself down, closed the curtains and threw the keys on the dining table before retiring to the master bedroom. He was snoring minutes after his head touched the pillow.

The driver of the car Stone had seen moving through the mountain hills was now making himself comfortable on an armchair in Daniel's lodge.

In complete darkness, he was carefully going over 'the plan'.

TUESDAY: DAY 8

FIFTY-THREE

Leaving her friends behind, she made her way to her car, the cool air in stark contrast to the warmth of the fashionable wine bar.

It was late, a lot later than she'd planned to stay out. She'd called home to apologise; her husband reassured her that everything was fine and to just enjoy herself. Her son was fast asleep. As she walked away towards the car park she smiled to herself. She didn't deserve a man like him.

In fact, she hadn't deserved her first husband either; they were both too good for her.

Her long silk designer dress ruffled around her ankles as a gust of cold night air swept past, revealing her black and white five-inch heels.

She'd enjoyed herself; it was good to catch up with some of her real friends, not the fake ones that so often attached themselves to her like leeches. She adored her life, her lifestyle and the money. It was so far removed from her upbringing in rural Worcestershire that she sometimes pinched herself to make sure it wasn't a dream.

Council-estate girl to WAG.

She thought that one day she might sit down and write her story: a rags-to-riches tale. She would just leave out the part where she had an affair behind the back of a man she loved. At least he'd moved on with his life; she just wished he would find a female companion and settle down. He deserved that. He deserved love.

She was startled by the sound of raised voices behind her: a young girl screaming profanities at her male companion who plodded onwards, oblivious to the tirade.

She shivered.

Natalie spun to face the sudden roar of an engine. Startled, she dropped her keys. As she bent to retrieve them, headlights illuminated her terrified face.

The car shot forward.

She saw the driver's door open at the last second and its impact thrust her into the air, the door used like a shield in a jousting tournament.

She lay in an awkward position, her left leg crushed underneath the right, both bent backwards at the knee. Her breathing became erratic as her lungs filled with blood. The outer layers of skin barely held her spine together.

She forced her eyes open as her attacker circled.

She was unable to move her neck so couldn't follow his complete orbit. With every circle the figure bent forward to inspect her, like a vulture making sure the prey was dead.

She closed her eyes and saw the face of her husband. She prayed that death would come quickly.

FIFTY-FOUR

Standing above her, one leg either side of her torso, he held the gun with a firm grip.

He remembered that he'd promised to do this slowly and painfully.

He watched her chest contract. He could hear the sound of fluid entering her respiratory system. He was no medical expert, but knew she didn't have long.

He needed to alter his plans. He hadn't meant the contact to be so catastrophic – only to knock her off her feet, certainly not to be crushed to death. He'd calculated incorrectly. The car door had collided with her head too forcefully and now he was going to have to adapt to the new situation. The game would be over before he'd really started having fun if she died now.

Her breathing stopped.

Shit.

He willed her to respond. God-damn it bitch – play the game!

A flicker from an eyelid or a drawn-out breath; there was nothing.

Fuck.

He had orchestrated his own downfall. Lost the game he invented, by being cocky.

He slammed his heel into her ribs and she let out a gasp.

There was only one thing left to do, and fast. He pulled hard on the trigger, and watched a spray of blood exit the puncture hole above her eyes.

He moved into action in one swift motion. His attention returned to the car as he fumbled with some items in the boot. After a few seconds he was back on the pavement above the body.

Natalie Gibbs, innocent victim of bullet number two. He could smell the blood on his gloves. The bullet had entered her forehead just off centre. It had penetrated tissue, fibre and bone. A pool of blood seeped out from the back of her head.

He moved fast to get her body into the boot. Once in, he took a jerry can out and poured water onto the blood on the road. It washed into the nearest drain.

He swung his car round, and onto the silent central ring road. He circled the town twice, then looked for the sign that he needed and took a left toward Kidderminster. He passed a few cars on his way; one was a patrol car.

He was fine – they wouldn't suspect anything yet.

FIFTY-FIVE

In the scheme of things, twenty minutes is not a great deal of time. When you're looking for car keys, however, it can feel like days.

Daniel was sure that when he'd gone to bed he'd left the keys on the kitchen table. They seemed to have evaporated. There wasn't a part of the cabin he hadn't searched: he felt in his pockets again, hoping that by some miracle they'd been there all along – that the previous five checks were rushed.

No, not there.

He retraced his steps for the eighth time. He opened the cabin door – it was unlocked and the keys were in the lock where he had left them.

Daniel remembered getting out immediately after his nonsensical conversation with the farmer. He'd dried off, changed for bed, thrown his keys on the dining table and gone to bed.

He did what all men would do in his situation and stood still on the spot.

For a lot of men this would be the point where a female companion entered the search and found the missing item within seconds. Daniel didn't have that luxury, so stood there a while longer. He'd lived alone for a few years, so had progressed to an advanced mode of thought. His evolution meant he questioned everything he'd ever been taught as a man, and to think like a woman instead.

It worked.

The car!

It was the only place he hadn't looked. He scooted across the wet decking, down the steps and opened the driver's door. The keys hung there almost as if to say, 'What kept you?'

Ten minutes later, Daniel was sitting in his car prepared for a day in the country; a walk somewhere, or a trip not too far to the sea. He put the car in reverse and moved off.

As he passed the farmhouse, Daniel saw the farmer and slowed so he could pass.

"Morning," the farmer said.

"Morning."

"You were in a hurry last night, tearing away from here like Lewis Hamilton."

Daniel could see that the farmer's eyes were bloodshot; no doubt he was hungover.

Maggie appeared at the door. "You were sick in the downstairs toilet last night," she said. "You need to clean that up."

She looked mad and, although he felt sorry for the farmer, Daniel didn't fancy elbowing in on a domestic; he nodded and smiled to both of them, then drove away.

FIFTY-SIX

Mud splattered across the back of her legs as her running shoes pounded the track. A week ago this route had been hard on her legs; the ground was dry and cracked then; now she needed to try hard to keep her balance in the slick mud.

She was just over an hour into her twice-weekly ten-mile workout. She'd made the journey along the River Severn to Stourport and had now twisted back toward the Georgian market-town of Bewdley. She was on the south side of the river now, where it was more rural; the north side had houses and apartments along it.

Here, there was just scrubland. Ahead of her in the distance stood the outline of riverside apartments, shops and the main bridge. To her right, a four-man rowing crew skimmed across the water. With every stroke, she saw the effort in their faces. She tried to match pace, but the ground put pay to that.

The track was thin at the best of times, but at this time of year, when vegetation was in full growth, it was more hazardous. She ducked her head beneath some bramble stems only to be hit on the cheek by a stray branch.

Her shoes were water-logged, and squelched with every stride. When she returned home she'd slip them off in her porch; hopefully they'd be dry for her Zumba class at eight.

There was a pause in the music on her phone as an automated female voice read out her current time, calories burnt, her distance of eight miles and her pace of seven minutes and thirty-two seconds. The voice finished and the track changed; the change lasted seconds longer than normal and jolted her concentration just enough that she lost her footing.

An Adele track softly played as she slid, her Lycra shorts no defence against the prickly environment she now found herself dumped in. Blisters broke out on her arms and legs and warm blood covered her right hand.

She eased herself painfully to her feet. Her right shin hurt. She looked down and felt faint. There was a good reason for the pain in her ankle. It took a minute or two for the sight to register in her mind, then she screamed. A five inch heel from a boot had pierced her skin and was lodged in her flesh. The sight of the wound was not what made her scream; she was a nurse and saw blood every day.

She screamed because the boot was still attached to a dismembered leg, running from the knee joint downwards.

FIFTY-SEVEN

Rhodes's office was dim; he had a light on but the fluorescent tube flickered. He looked up at it and shook his head. Once this meeting was over he'd send another email to maintenance, his fifth so far. Until then he had to dodge the health and safety rep just in case the subject of adequate lighting and its ill-effects resurfaced.

He was the only one in work.

He had gone to bed earlier than normal and had subsequently arrived at work earlier. He wasn't tired – he was ready. Today, Rhodes was finally going to put Alex Burns in a prison cell and slam the door on him for a long time.

All he needed was proof. That was the hard part.

Alex, of course, knew the system; he knew that Rhodes had seven, maybe eight hours maximum, before he was charged or released.

Time was ticking.

The knock on his office door made him physically jump.

He looked up to see Tammy Cavendish, her hair a mess, her make-up gone. She had been crying; her eyes were swollen and red, and a mark covered most of her left cheek.

Rhodes took her in. Though pale and tired, without her makeup there was an innocence about her, a natural, girl-next-door look.

"Miss Cavendish, can I help you?"

Tammy entered the room, took a seat and placed a mobile phone on the desk. It was an iPhone. It had scratches all over it, but Rhodes could see it still worked.

"I am here to show you who killed Abbie Flynn."

Rhodes let her speak.

After ten minutes he felt like her shrink. When he'd asked her to start at the beginning he hadn't expected her to literally start at the very beginning, right from the moment her father had ripped them away from their lives in Liverpool one cold Wednesday night.

Rhodes didn't stop her, though. No matter how long it took, he wanted to know who'd killed Abbie Flynn; if it meant hearing this girl's life story, so be it.

"I don't understand," he broke in.

"Understand what?" she snapped.

Rhodes watched her eyes; she wouldn't look at him. The whole time she had been re-living her tormented life, she hadn't looked up.

"From what you tell me, Tammy, you've been part of a family that doesn't get on too well with the law. So why are you here, why now?"

Their eyes met for the first time.

"I'm not a grass, and my father need never know. I need to tell you because I'm worried this monster will attack someone else. Maybe me next time."

"But I still don't understand – if you knew who it was over a week ago, why not tell us then?"

"I felt sorry for her family; I saw her mom in the supermarket yesterday before everything kicked off at the pub. She looked like she needed closure."

"So you see yourself as a modern day Molly Malone."

Tammy looked puzzled.

"The tart with the heart. Don't worry, wrong generation. So what can you tell me that we don't already know?"

Tammy went to pocket her phone.

"Sorry, I shouldn't have said that. If you can help I would be grateful."

She thumbed through the icons on her phone and stopped at the video gallery. "I don't need to tell you, Detective Rhodes – I need to show you." She started the recording.

Rhodes watched intently. His eyes tightened as the sound of a young female's screams filled his office. Then it all stopped. He closed his eyes for a beat and took a few deep breaths.

"Thank you, Miss Cavendish. You've done the right thing."

FIFTY-EIGHT

Crooks and DS Bates bounced questions off one another in an attempt to generate an idea - an idea which they could then use to produce a theory, a theory that just might produce a motive, a motive that would, of course, lead to an arrest and conviction.

Joel Murray listened in on their conversation while thinking up some questions of his own.

"Why now?" said Bates.

"Why not?"

"Like I said, it doesn't make sense. This guy grew up watching a father beat all kinds of crap out of his mother. He did nothing. Then he watches his father, mother and brother die one by one, in the space of three years. Evidence says he stayed well within the law. His wife walks out, takes his son and sets up home with another man. Yet a full six years later he loses his job, and that suddenly flips him and he turns psycho killer. I don't get it."

"What about the bang he took to the head? There have been numerous cases of personality change because the person received a head injury. Although, it would have to have happened very quickly, I have to admit."

"Yeah, it was a minute and half after he took the bang to the head before the attack on Abbie Flynn."

Murray spoke up. "It's all to do with resistance."

"What?"

Murray scanned his desk and picked up a thirty-centimetre ruler. "This is shatter-resistant, right?"

Murray loved an audience. He loved theorising and a lot of the time he was right, which was why he was so well-respected in the force. Flexing the ruler between his fingers, he continued. "Not shatter-proof, just like Daniel Stone. Each event in his life flexed him a little more, but didn't change him. Like this ruler. He carried on with his daily routine without incident. Watch, the childhood, then the brother..." Murray gave the ruler a harder flex with each event in Stone's life. "Each event weakened him until, at last, he lost his job and –" The ruler snapped in half. "He snapped!"

Murray took his seat and started to work on his computer. Filled with pride, he'd almost convinced himself he was correct.

The room fell silent for a minute or so then Bates spoke.

"Bullshit!"

Murray didn't reply.

"You heard DCI Graham; Daniel Stone is as clean as they come. I bet the guy even cries at the sob story VTs on XFactor."

Murray looked up. "Everything has a breaking point. It's a common law of physics. It's just how things are made, and humans are no exception. I have a feeling Rhodes suspects Stone."

"No, some people are made differently – you can throw as much shit at them as you like and they wash it off and carry on."

"Maybe he just ran out of water this time. I saw him too. I rarely listen to the words. I try to watch the eyes, see what they communicate, and there's something hiding behind Daniel Stone's eyes. Fifty quid says he's got more to do with the two deaths than you think."

"I understand what you're saying, but I'm going for this Tesar guy."

The conversation halted as Inspector Rhodes burst into the room. He dashed over the boards and pulled the photo of Daniel Stone off the information board and threw it in the bin. He was smiling, buoyant.

"Listen up; we now have two separate investigations. We have Abbie Flynn's killer, so everything's changed."

The men gathered around their boss.

He hadn't been in his office when they'd arrived. His light had been on, so they knew he was somewhere close. Now they were about to find out exactly what he'd been doing.

FIFTY-NINE

Alex Burns looked tired as he sat at the table in Interview Room Two.

Across from him were Tori Vilani and Patrick Rhodes. Vilani was dressed in a navy trouser-suit, her hair brushed back and secured into a ponytail with a pink bobble. Rhodes was dressed in the same suit from the day before, but unlike Burns he looked like he'd had a decent night's sleep.

The door opened and a uniformed officer let Ainsworth in. He scurried around and took the seat next to Alex, opened his briefcase and fumbled for a pen and paper.

The smell of instant coffee filled the room. Rhodes motioned with his eyes toward the coffee that sat in a Thermos mug in front of the solicitor. Vilani smiled back.

"Shall we begin?" he asked.

He looked directly at the solicitor who gazed back, giving a sheepish nod.

Rhodes looked at Alex Burns. There was no response from him; the solicitor nodded on his behalf.

Rhodes announced who was present for the tape and began. "We said a lot of things yesterday, so I'll keep it brief today. I know Alex needs to get away to collect his wife from the airport." The sarcasm was registered by everyone present. Rhodes proceeded to reach into his pocket and retrieved a mobile phone. "For the benefit of the tape, I am about to show Mr. Burns a video that came into police possession early this morning. I will advise how this recording came into our possession once we've all seen it."

"If it's the one with your wife in, don't bother. I've seen it," Alex said, his eyes still fixed on the floor. The skin in the corner of his thumb was red and sore where he had picked at it during the previous interview. He started to pick at it again.

Rhodes just grinned and played the video.

He'd seen it, so he knew what was coming. He wanted to watch as the smirk was wiped off Burns's face. For the longest time now, Rhodes had regretted having done nothing to stop his niece from marrying this beast; now he didn't have to. Burns had put an end to it himself.

The video was grainy and dark. It showed a fight taking place between a woman and a man. The man wasn't recognisable; the woman was Abbie Flynn. She fought hard to free herself from her attacker.

Alex looked on unmoved; still no expression, even as the screaming grew louder.

Then a second man was seen on the screen.

The man tried to fend off the girl's attacker. He eventually managed to do so and the first man fled.

A car drove past and blocked the lens for a second. The detective paused the recording.

The room was silent, save for the whirring sound from the tape recorder.

Alex looked up gradually until his eyes met Rhodes's.

"You're going to try and say that's me?"

"No, I know full well who that is, and don't worry, I'll deal with him soon enough," replied Rhodes, shaking his head.

"You're losing your touch, old man. You used to chase after us as kids, now you lot want to pin all kinds of crap on us. You should get that vintage video out later. The one where a detective chased a gang into the old sugar-beet site and nearly ended up dead. I like that one."

The finger that had paused the video clip now pressed down on the play function. The clip started once more from where it had been stopped.

The picture was clear again, as the car moved on. The second man had disappeared; Abbie Flynn sobbed hysterically, obviously bewildered as she reached down to rescue her bag from the gutter. At this point a car sped onto the screen in reverse, smashing into Abbie Flynn.

Alex dropped his head into his hands.

Like his enemy across the table, he knew what was coming. The only person oblivious was Ainsworth.

The video was paused again.

"You want to tell me what happens next?" asked Rhodes.

Burns tried one last attempt at bravado. "On *A Question of Sport* now, are we?"

No one smiled. Burns hung his head.

Rhodes continued with the video.

He could feel the adrenaline pumping through his body. In a few seconds' time all the rubbish police life threw at him would disappear. This was why he had chosen to become a detective over twenty years ago. He felt about ten feet tall.

The video played on and from out of the car stepped Alex Burns. He crouched to the rear of his car, hovering inches above Abbie's body. He shook his head, looked around and ran back to his car and sped away.

"You left her."

"It was an accident."

"I saw her fighting with the other man. I wanted to help, I reversed, but —"

"But what?"

"I reversed too fast and hit her as she bent down."

"Why did you drive off, Alex, if it was an accident? Why didn't you call an ambulance?" Vilani asked.

"I don't know, I really don't. Look, I'm not that man any more. I've changed. I made a mistake. I don't know why I left her there."

Rhodes shuffled in his chair. "I do."

Burns raised his head to hear what the detective was about say.

"I know, you know, and Tammy Cavendish could tell when she videoed this. Tell us, Alex, why you drove away when it was *clearly* an accident."

Burns slumped down further in his chair

"Shall I put us all out of our misery? You drove away because —"

"I was drunk. I was fucking drunk, I'd been drinking all night. But you knew that yesterday. That's what all the shit with football scores was about. You're a bastard, Rhodes; I should have killed you when I had the chance!" Alex yelled as the realisation that Rhodes had finally got him hit home.

There was a moment of silence before Rhodes spoke again, his words calm and professional now. This was no time to gloat. He had a new problem. If Alex Burns had been responsible for Abbie Flynn's death, then who killed Mackenzie Rogers?

"I did know you'd done it. I just needed the proof, which I told you I'd get. Alex Burns, I am charging you with the death of Miss Abbie Flynn, and with driving under the influence."

SIXTY

There was just one parking space vacant on the Mercury Business Park, a farm conversion on the northern outskirts of Kidderminster, which, so far, housed only two businesses.

The main farmhouse and two large barns constituted the site of Flynn Carson Ltd., and Print Kings worked from the remaining couple of smaller out-buildings. Rhodes wasn't interested in the Print Kings offices; he headed for the main farmhouse.

He opened an original stable door and entered the offices. Once inside he wondered why they had kept the outside looking so traditional, while inside the architects had removed all evidence of a working farm. Slick plastered walls, shimmering polished wooden floors, and a fish tank that a sea-life centre would be envious of created a glamorous reception area. Rhodes hated it instantly, just like the franchise pubs he detested.

He approached the reception desk and was greeted by an aroma of fresh coffee and expensive perfume. Both came via an attractive receptionist who looked at him now with a forced smile. Young women rarely smiled at him.

"Can I help you, sir?" she said with a purr.

"I'm here to see Mr. Flynn. Detective Inspector Patrick Rhodes." He flashed his card.

The expression on her face changed. There was sadness in her eyes.

It puzzled Rhodes for a second, then he realised what was going on. The attractive receptionist in front of him was a little closer to her boss than she should be. Just the mention of his name reminded her of their relationship and possibly the guilt of it, affected by recent events.

The girl dialed a number and informed Gregory Flynn that Rhodes was here.

"He'll be straight down."

He didn't have to wait long before Gregory Flynn arrived. He smiled but, like the receptionist, the smile seemed forced. He was dressed in a slim-fitting grey suit, much more expensive than Rhodes's. Rhodes had never felt comfortable in a suit. He wore one every day and looked reasonably good in them, but he'd much rather throw on some jeans and a T-shirt.

They shook hands. A gold watch slipped into view, glinting in the light.

"Detective Rhodes."

"Mr. Flynn. How are you?"

"What do you think, Detective? My daughter is dead and my wife has left me."

Rhodes noticed the receptionist quickly look up at Flynn and back to her work, confirming his earlier suspicions.

"You'd best be here to give me the name and address of the man who killed my daughter, so I can keep my promise to her."

"You know I can't do that, Mr. Flynn. However, I can tell you I have charged the man responsible."

"Do you have children, Detective?"

"Yes, a daughter, so I know how you feel."

"She alive?"

"She is."

"Then you have no idea how I feel. You're going to charge this man, and he will spend a few years of his life in rent-free accommodation being waited on three times a day. Do you know what my little girl will be doing while this happens?"

Rhodes chose not to answer; the years had taught him not to further enrage the grief-stricken.

"She will be decomposing."

Rhodes remained silent. He'd worked out early on in his career that he best thing to do with grieving relatives was to let them talk. Talking made them feel better; they didn't know it, but it did.

"That bastard will be free before my son gets to Abbie's age."

Gregory Flynn carried on ranting, and Rhodes appeared to be listening, but his phone was vibrating over and over. Someone was in a hurry to speak to him.

"Mr. Flynn, I am extremely sorry for your loss. I wanted to let you know first before we release the information to the press. If there is anything you need from the police, please contact me."

As he opened the door to leave, Rhodes was questioned once more by Greg Flynn.

"You ever find the person that got on my drive that night?"

Out of sight, Rhodes grinned.

Three Bullets

"I know who it was, and don't worry, he'll know that I know very soon."

SIXTY-ONE

"Okay, so you have the Flynn girl's killer, but can I just add that you've been chasing shadows all along. I have a feeling Jakub Tesar is gone and we might never find him. Now sort this out, Rhodes!"

John Graham was angry, and he wanted Rhodes to know it.

Rhodes went to speak but stopped himself; he didn't take too kindly to being screamed at in his own office. It was disrespectful; even more so when his team were in earshot. Rhodes took his time forming his response – this wasn't the time to say what he actually wanted to; that would keep. But he needed to say something.

"Yes, Sir."

Rhodes's phone vibrated on his desk. It was his wife. She'd be getting on a plane in an hour, and he couldn't wait to see her. He'd missed her. He let it ring; he didn't want to have to tell her about Alex.

There was a knock at the door. It was Murray, looking flustered and not his usual confident, bordering on arrogant, self.

"Sorry to bother you, Sir, but I think we have another problem. I was searching the database and spotted a call logged this morning from a Tom Gibbs. Misper."

Misper was police talk for missing person.

"Seems his wife went out last night and didn't return."

Graham spoke angrily. "With all due respect, DS Murray, we have more pressing things to deal with than some woman that's a bit bored with her husband and has pulled an all–nighter!"

Rhodes took no notice of his boss. "Get someone to Daniel Stone's house now and arrest him."

"Yes, sir."

"Excuse me, Rhodes, but am I missing something?"

He felt like saying *always, Sir, you're always missing something* but he paused for breath. Thinking before speaking wasn't something he regularly did.

"Tom Gibbs is a premiership footballer. His wife is Natalie Gibbs, previously Natalie Stone."

"So?"

"Sir, do I have to spell it out for you? Firstly, we have a prominent businessman's daughter dead, an international bestselling author dead and, if I'm right, we could have one of the most high profile WAGs in the Midlands missing. More importantly, Natalie Stone is the ex-wife of *Daniel* Stone. If she's missing, with the week we've had, I bet you your annual salary she'll turn up dead."

"I wouldn't take that bet, sir," said Murray. "She's been found, and Rhodes is right – she turned up dead all right. Bullet to the head, just like Mackenzie."

"Back to your earlier point, Sir, regarding Jakub Tesar. Well, I think Joel is going to confirm why we've let him slip through our fingers – am I right, Sergeant?"

"We checked out a few things regarding Natalie Gibbs and it seems she was out with friends last night; her car is still in the car park where she left it."

"So?" Graham said.

"So I did some detecting, like you keep telling us to do. Guess whose car registration appeared on five ANPR cameras across the area?"

"Daniel Stone's?" Graham guessed.

Murray didn't answer; he just followed Rhodes out of his office.

The scene down at the riverside was a mess.

Rhodes had spent plenty of time near water as a policeman. Suicides, accidents and murders: corpses seem to be attracted to the River Severn. Water was dangerous at the best of times and a lot of the time the water in this area was not at its best.

The runner who'd discovered the boot was sitting on the step of an ambulance. She had a towel draped around her and was in conversation with an officer.

Rhodes walked past her. She was of no use to him. All she could tell him was that she found a boot with a leg in it. It would have probably taken her well over ten minutes to tell him that because there was no doubt that at certain points in her recollection she would turn into a blubbering, hysterical wreck.

Rhodes was interested in the rest of the body, which had been found thirty minutes later further along the bank. He took a walk with Murray to where two black bags lay on the ground; a man was taking photos.

They didn't get too close before another man, dressed in full protective gear, joined them from the riverside. Coroner Ray Bullen.

"Definitely her, Ray?" asked Rhodes.

"Not had a formal identification yet, but she had a few distinguishing marks, not to mention quite a unique wedding ring. We've matched it all against records and I can say I'm pretty much one hundred percent."

"Okay, so how do you think this happened?"

"It didn't happen here. We have a team searching the area near where her car was found. It seems she was shot in the head at the roadside and then brought here. There was some serious damage done before the shooting. I'll need to do a full investigation, but my instincts tell me that her killer mowed her down with a car and then shot her. There are two things I don't understand, though."

"Just two? You're getting better in your old age, Ray."

"First, why shoot her? Her injuries would have killed her. And secondly, why dismember her?"

"Did the attacker use a saw for the leg?"

"Again, I can't tell for sure yet; however, if you do find the car, I'd check the boot. I'd say that the attacker slammed the boot down on her leg to snap it off."

Murray and Rhodes looked at each other. Rhodes shook Ray Bullen's gloved hand and the pair returned to his Audi. "This can't be Daniel Stone, Patrick. He's not capable of this. Is he?" Murray tried to sound confident.

He wasn't, and Rhodes could tell.

"You said it yourself, his car popped up all over the place. I think he's been one step ahead of us, but he won't be any more. I'll get the son of a bitch."

Rhodes followed the lane back into town. He slowed as he crossed the bridge over the Severn and took a quick look up and down the river. This little town was such a wonderful picture-postcard riverside town.

What had made Stone dump Natalie's body there?

Why had he just left her on the riverbank?

There was something wrong with the whole thing. It would have been easier to dump the body in the river. It would have washed maybe thirty miles downstream, or disappeared somewhere into the sea way past Bristol if it had picked up a good undercurrent.

If this was Daniel Stone, then he wasn't doing this with any conviction.

Rhodes followed the one road out of Bewdley back towards Kidderminster.

SIXTY-TWO

Twenty chairs were laid out in rows of five. These had filled up straight away, and people were beginning to gather around the edges of the presentation room. Rhodes had expected a bit more interest than usual due to identities of the two individuals on the mortuary table – an international bestselling author and the wife of one of English football's brightest stars.

Rhodes, Graham and Vilani took in the news teams in front of them. There were representatives from at least four TV news stations, national and local radio, tabloid and local newspaper journalists.

Rhodes liked what he saw; he knew a few of them and could see an eagerness to get the story out. That could help catch Stone, making it difficult for him to hide. Take his feeble little face and plaster it all over the media, so that it became the most recognized face in the country. He wanted to dislodge the latest half-naked celebrity from the cover of those weekly mags and make Daniel Stone the national topic of conversation.

The room fell silent save for the snap of flashing cameras. DCI Graham addressed them.

"Thank you all for coming this morning. Some of you will know me, some of you won't. I'm DCI John Graham. I will be very brief. DI Rhodes will provide you with as much detail as we can give at present, then he will take three questions."

Graham sat back – he'd done his bit and showed his face to the public. He was new to the role, which helped – he hadn't yet promised things and failed to deliver. People in the area still trusted him.

"Thank you, sir." Rhodes spoke with confidence. "Today we have charged a man with the killing of Abbie Flynn. I can also confirm that the body of the female found on the riverbank in Bewdley is that of Mrs. Natalie Gibbs. Evidence has come to light that allows us to confirm that the two deaths are unrelated. Evidence does, however, suggest that there is a link between the homicide of Roger Mackenzie and Natalie Gibbs. We would like to question a Mr. Daniel Stone, who was last seen in the Kidderminster area yesterday."

Rhodes paused for a minute as he held up an A3 photo of Daniel Stone to the camera crews. "We do not know his present whereabouts, and would urge anyone who has seen him, or has any relevant information, to contact the force immediately. Thank you."

A young man dressed in a sharp suit raised his hand: "Do you think there will be more killings?"

"Not if we get the help we need from the public."

A question from three rows back. "What are the reasons for these killings?"

"That's what we're currently working on."

A question from the front row. Rhodes knew this reporter well: Gillian Grant, the head reporter for the local paper, the one most households in the area got free every

Thursday. There had been a few run-ins with Grant over the years, but never any grudges. He used her when he needed her, and today her customers would be his biggest allies.

"Is it true that the link you mentioned is that both victims were murdered with a single bullet to the head, and, if so, is the gun still on the streets?"

"Technically, that's two questions, Gillian."

There was a ripple of laughter. Grant gave an innocent shrug.

"I'll answer you like this. At present we do not have the gun. Daniel Stone is a very dangerous man. It is our duty to protect the public and that is what we intend to do. There is a tendency for people to turn a blind eye to crime because it's safer not to get involved. Sometimes it may seem that way, but not in this case, not with a man like this. I ask you to print the name Daniel Stone in your papers. Do it however you like, but do it so that people see it. Do it so your readers and viewers know who this man is. If you see Daniel Stone, do not approach him, contact us and let us do our job. That is all, thank you."

A few more journalists called out, one annoying question coming from Richard Clough, which Rhodes ignored, and a camera or two flashed.

Rhodes and the other police present rose from their seats and made their way to the exit. The room transformed into a frenzy of activity; people turned to their phones, trying to beat the journalist next to them to breaking the story, while camera crews worked hard to download and edit footage on the move.

SIXTY-THREE

The petrol gauge on Daniel Stone's dashboard hung curiously above the empty line. He was confused; he'd put over fifty pounds worth of fuel in the tank less than a day ago. More worrying was it had only been thirty or so miles away.

He looked at the road ahead and tried to familiarise himself with the surroundings. He had not been this way for a while. What he needed was a signpost, a mile maker, a pub he remembered, say.

What he got were fields, framed on all sides by mountains.

The sky looked as though someone had drawn it with a piece of charcoal and then smudged the paper with wet cotton wool.

The petrol gauge dropped a millimeter or two more, though Daniel tried to be a little more economical with the accelerator. Ahead there were a few dark buildings. They looked like they were made from stone, with slate roofs. A farm, maybe. As the car got closer Daniel saw a 'Children crossing' sign and two amber globes blinking on either side of the road. A school. A school meant there must be houses, maybe a convenience store, and possibly a petrol station.

Two miles later, Daniel's hopes were confirmed.

There were houses, a convenience store, and even two pubs, The Kings Head and The Farmers Arms, neither of which sold petrol. One place in the village did sell fuel though – the tractor dealership.

'Dealership' was an optimistic description. They had one model of tractor on the forecourt. Daniel was not interested in the tractor, anyway – he was interested in the three pumps out in front of the main building. Daniel filled his car and went inside. The shop smelt of oil and microwaved pasties.

There was a queue of three people at the counter. A middle-aged man was first in line, his green trousers drenched in slurry. Second was a young mum, fighting to keep control of an over-active child who still hadn't grasped the meaning of the word no. Finally, Daniel Stone, waiting to pay for the packet of mints he gripped in his hand, and his petrol.

As he shuffled forward, he tried to figure out how he'd used three-quarters of a tank of petrol in half a day. He had a friend who tinkered with cars in his spare time, so he would drop in on him when he was back in Kidderminster. Maybe he'd a split a pipe.

The farmer paid and exited the shop. The mother took a few minutes to convince her boy that chocolate buttons were not a good idea this early in the morning, then she paid.

Daniel placed the mints on the counter and smiled. He had learnt to try and look as friendly as he could, to take the focus away from his facial injuries.

Behind the counter stood a lad in his late twenties; behind him was a tiny TV. It was flashing as two policemen walked away from the screen. The lad switched it off.

"What's going on?"

The lad ignored Stone's question.

"The police – anything serious?"

Daniel entered his PIN into the machine and waited for the receipt.

"You from England? One of your overpaid footballers' wives has been killed," the lad said.

He said it in such a way that he distanced himself from any involvement in it. YOUR overpaid footballers. An English person, not Welsh.

Daniel's heart sank. "Did they say which one?"

"I think so, but aren't they all the same?"

"I meant the wife; can you put it back on?"

The boy looked around at the tiny blank screen and then back at Stone. He shook his head. "No, this is a petrol station, not a cinema. All I know is the police are after her ex-husband."

"Why?" There was serious panic in Daniel's tone.

"Think he's dangerous, killed some old bloke as well."

Daniel stumbled to the car.

He had suddenly worked out the petrol consumption puzzle. Jakub Tesar had followed him, used his car to drive back to Kidderminster and kill Natalie. The bonnet of his car just about held his weight as he failed to stand.

The world was crashing down around him. He wasn't safe anywhere – he had to fight this head on. There hadn't been a third name; Daniel guessed what might happen if a third name didn't materialise.

He needed to get home.

Three Bullets

Rhodes wanted him, Tesar wanted him – the only way to win this was to bring these two men together so they could sort each other out. First he had to get to Ollie – he would be in torment, with his mother dead and his father the number one suspect.

SIXTY-FOUR

Sitting in his car just under half a mile from Tom Gibbs's house, Daniel thought over his plan. There was no way he could get anywhere near the property; he could see the flashing lights above the hedgerows further down the hill.

In truth he was astonished he'd gotten this far; surely his registration plate would have been picked up by one of those ANPR cameras he kept hearing about.

It didn't matter – he was here now.

A sheep nudged its nose through an ageing fence, inspecting the newest resident of the lay-by.

His first reaction was to give himself up, but they'd never believe him; he was having trouble believing himself.

A travelling Czech salesman saved his life, only to drag him into his sick and twisted game, which had culminated in three people's lives being taken. And now this mystery Czech was nowhere to be found.

Anyway, he'd chosen the names; he'd written them down. It was his handwriting on the piece of paper which Tesar, no doubt, was still in possession of.

Daniel tried to get a hold on his emotions; he wanted to speak to his son so much. The thought of what Ollie must be going through raked at his heart. Many years ago his own dad had been his hero until he realised why his mom cried so much. In that moment he had come to understand that his father was a bad man.

Ollie must be thinking the same now.

Daniel over-compensated a lot of the time, trying to make up for the failure of not being there every day, and questioned whether he sometimes did more harm to their relationship by seeking constant reassurance that Ollie loved him.

There was no doubt that Ollie hated him now.

Daniel turned the key hard in the ignition and circled the car back away from the house. There was a new plan, and this one had to work.

*

For most of the five minute journey his eyes were fixed on the rearview mirror; no police so far, a good thing.

Parking his car two streets away from Stourbridge Junction railway station, he was strangely calm. He locked the car and dropped to his knees, fiddling with his shoelace. He began to loosen the grip on his car keys until they dropped into the drain next to him. With a loud plop, they were gone.

Daniel chose to walk the last hundred or so yards to the ticket office; there must be CCTV in the car park, and he didn't want his number plate being picked up, not yet anyway.

He asked the lady in the ticket booth if there was a pay phone; she exaggeratedly pointed to its location at the front of the building.

He'd missed it, which was not good. He needed to switch on; if they were treating him like a criminal then he needed to act like one. He couldn't believe how easily he'd slipped into this new role, having never really wanted to break the law and always imagining that it was difficult to do so.

He made a call, then returned to the ticket office and purchased a single ticket to Kidderminster, paying cash. He waited a while on the platform for the train to arrive then watched the doors open. A few people got off, pushing past the ones who rushed to get on.

Daniel stood watching as the train pulled away before turning and returning down the stairs, passing the ticket office, keeping his head down so the attendant did not see him, and out to the car park where his taxi was waiting. He opened the door and got in.

"Kidderminster, please."

The taxi driver gave a nod, and casually accelerated.

"Wait!"

The driver stopped.

"No, sorry, carry on," Daniel said, closing the passenger door behind him.

SIXTY-FIVE

The interview room was full of uniformed officers, detectives and volunteers. Some were on duty, while others had been called in to provide back-up. This was, in theory, a manhunt.

"A patrol unit has found his car," Jackie Roberts announced.

An excited wave of anticipation rippled through the room.

Rhodes allowed a small smile to escape.

"Where?" asked Murray.

"Parked near Stourbridge Junction station," Roberts replied, taking a seat next to Bates.

"We need to get a team down to Kidderminster station and arrest him as he gets off – do you want me to go, sir?" Bates asked.

"Already done, sir," added Roberts proudly.

"No, that's too simple. We need to get the CCTV from the platform in Stourbridge and make sure he got on that train, or indeed if he even went to the station." Rhodes was wary of jumping to conclusions – if Stone was coming home, it was too easy for him to just hop on a train and turn up at his door. He'd already given them the run-around all week; a few more days would be no mean feat.

"Got officers going through them, sir."

Rhodes turned to Janet Beevers, the press officer. A lady in her mid-twenties, she wore wire-rimmed glasses; Rhodes often wondered if they were for show more than necessity. As she titled her head to listen to him, her treacle-coloured hair fell across her face.

"Janet, we need you to put out another press release informing the public that Daniel Stone has been spotted in Stourbridge. We believe he is attempting to return to the Kidderminster area. Inform the public if they see this man to contact us straight away and do not approach him as he may be armed."

Janet nodded and made a note on her pad.

Murray leaned forward and spoke. "Sir, I have a theory."

"Shoot."

"I got hold of his bank records and he withdrew three hundred pounds from an ATM in Welshpool high street at ten-thirty yesterday, then three hundred from the same ATM this morning at eleven. Nothing since. We need to make sure his hasn't got his passport on him. Six hundred pounds is a decent amount of money if he wants to run. I say put the airports on alert."

Rhodes pondered Murray's theory for little under thirty seconds before he rubbished it. "No, I've met him, and I don't think he has a proper plan. It's more likely he'll hide out and, hopefully, try to make contact with his son."

Roberts' phone rang. The other detectives discussed some more information, half listening to Roberts' end of the conversation. She hung up and smiled uneasily.

"Seems we have our man, sir – all we need to do is find him. A gun and a grey suit jacket were found on the back seat of his car. The jacket had a balled-up piece of paper in the inside pocket with two names scribbled on it." She looked around the table. "Anyone fancy guessing whose names they were?"

No one did – they all knew the answer.

Robert's phone rang again. The tone was a long computerized stream. No tune. No words.

"Hello?"

She had the attention of everyone in the room as she listened to the caller.

"Okay, that's great, keep it coming. Bye." She looked at Rhodes sitting at the head of the table.

"They opened his boot, like you asked sir."

"And?"

"Blood. There's blood everywhere. There are fragments of bone and tissue in the locking system too."

Rhodes nodded in acknowledgement of the good work.

SIXTY-SIX

The money was running out fast; he lay out what remained on the bed, making a mental note to be more careful.

On the dressing table, a tiny kettle clicked off.

He needed to start thinking straight. Sixty pounds on this damp, musty room. The police should arrest the fragile looking middle-aged lady – with little in the way of personality and lots of decorative china – for extortion.

She'd told him in her monotone voice that breakfast was served between seven and eight – no later, or he'd go hungry.

Daniel took a sip of his complimentary tea and he took another look around the room; expensive it may have been but it was exactly what he needed right now. He opened the curtains. The view didn't make the price any more reasonable: the bricks of the next house, and, if he strained his neck, a glimpse of the busy road beyond.

The window was large, allowing a good deal of light in; this made the room look bigger, but also illuminated more of the inexcusable décor. The worst culprit was a floral cloth on a bedside table. A stained beige lamp sat atop a lace doily, finishing the whole mess off. Daniel questioned whether any one still made, or bought, doilies.

He questioned once more what the hell he was doing. He wasn't here to sip tea from a china cup whilst mulling over the finer details of interior design; he was here to drag himself out of the pile of crap his life had so quickly become.

Daniel thought he had a plan.

But he really didn't; he just wanted to see his son, and that was never going to happen. Now, with no idea what to do next, he slumped against the window.

*

A little later Daniel peeled his face off the cold surface and made his way along the hallway to the only bathroom on the second floor.

He questioned his decision-making once more. Sixty pounds for a room with no en-suite? What was he thinking?

He locked the door and started to run a bath; the water choked out through the ancient piping and spluttered into the enamel tub.

There was a knock at a door along the hallway, followed by the landlady calling out a man's name. For a second, the name she was shouting didn't quite sink in – when it did, Daniel panicked. Another knock sounded and the lady spoke again.

"Mr. Tesar, I have some towels for you."

There was one final knock; this one was on the bathroom door. "Sorry to bother you – forgot to say earlier. Breakfast is served seven till eight, not one minute over. You're late, you go without, okay?"

Daniel stayed silent; she'd told him this earlier, near enough word for word. Why was she telling him again?

Was it to get him to speak, so Jakub Tesar would hear his voice, come barging in and use bullet number three? Fearful, he turned the tap off. He needed to get out of here and quickly.

SIXTY-SEVEN

Rhodes leaned against Murray's metallic-blue Vauxhall Astra. Murray, standing a few feet away, had his mobile glued to his ear once again.

"Where are you, Daniel Stone?" Rhodes said.

Murray ended his call and turned to his boss. "Might have something, sir. Master spoke to the taxi firm Stone used to get from the station. Seems he did attempt to come home. Driver says he gave him his address, but as they turned into the road, he changed his mind and asked to be dropped somewhere else. Taxi driver believes the police presence changed his mind."

"Where did he go?"

"Here's the strange thing: the driver says he felt that Stone didn't seem to know where he wanted to go, then suddenly as he was driving towards the cricket club, Stone says, this'll do, and jumps out."

"What's at the cricket ground, Joel?"

"Stumps me, sir," smiled Murray.

Rhodes tried not to smile. He was trying hard to picture the roads around the cricket ground.

"Let's have a drive, see if we can see what he saw."

"Only if we can take your car, sir."

*

Kidderminster Cricket Club was located on Chester Road, long stretch of road that formed part of a network of roads which connected Worcester with Wolverhampton. Kidderminster sat almost in the middle. Chester Road itself was a long Roman-style road; predominately residential, with a high school, a couple of pubs and the cricket club.

The first pass of the club left them blank. They had travelled from the south so the cricket club had been on the right. They headed back past with the club on the left. Still nothing. Houses, flats. Owned and rented. A bed and breakfast. Some more houses.

Rhodes slowed the car. "Joel, we need to get every B&B and hotel checked. He was coming home, maybe for a passport like you said, or maybe he has more money hidden, but because we have officers here, he panicked. I think he's hiding somewhere, and no better place than a B&B or hotel."

"How many B&Bs are there?"

"On this road, two. In the Kidderminster area, a damn sight more. We'll start here though; maybe we'll get lucky."

Rhodes pulled his car into a side street and parked tight to the curb. The street was narrow and he didn't want to return to a scrape along his new Audi.

They emerged onto Chester Road and split up. Rhodes took an establishment named Rosie's Villa. Murray got the imaginatively named Chester Road B&B.

It didn't take Rhodes long to re-appear on to the main road. The economic crisis had started to hit Rosie. She had no guests at all. She half joked that even a murderer would be welcome at the moment. Rhodes hadn't found it funny.

Murray had a little more luck. He had been greeted by a lady in her mid-thirties. She told him they had five guests, four men and one woman. Two were train enthusiasts, here to see the Severn Valley railway. She seemed proud of the town's main tourist attraction. Then there was the woman, who was in town on business. So, in fact, was the third man, who was some sort of salesman. The fourth man, she had no idea – he booked in early while she was at the wholesalers getting breakfast supplies. The lady called her mother, the owner, in from the garden.

"Hi, I'm Detective Joel Murray. I need your current guest list, if possible."

The elderly lady looked skeptical at first but agreed and went to the office to fetch it.

Rhodes's phone beeped. He answered it automatically.
"Rhodes."

He listened and then ended the call. He looked left and right before darting across the road. He burst into the reception of the Chester Road B&B and shouted for Murray.

"They have him. He's at Crossely Retail Park. He's on foot and he's running. Come on."

When the lady returned the policeman was gone. Only her daughter stood in the corridor.

"They've found him. I don't think we need the guest book any more," she said to her mother.

SIXTY-EIGHT

The chimes of a bell tower struck four. In between each one distant sirens faded in and out. Daniel raced across the dull tarmac of the superstore car park. Around him he could hear the sirens getting louder, closer. There were so many, it was hard to tell which direction they were approaching from. He knew one thing, though – that they weren't coming from the direction he was headed; not unless they had police barges.

In the distance, lights caught his eyes and a police car jostled for a way through the afternoon traffic. Daniel darted away in the opposite direction, and came close to having his kneecaps crushed by the plastic bumper of an oncoming Nissan.

A minute later he was on a gravel towpath; he calculated the pros and cons of the directions now open to him.

Ahead of him was the canal itself – he mentally crossed that off his list; there was just foliage on the other side and he didn't want to get wet; that would only slow him down.

The direction from which he had come was not a good choice. So, just left and right remained. He took a long look to the right. On the opposite side of the canal stood the magnificent St Mary's Church. Beyond that a road bridge, and further in the distance, the town centre of Kidderminster. Retail parks, shops, passageways and crowds of people, all great places to get lost in.

Daniel had half made his mind up when he remembered the TV bulletin; he wouldn't be able to hide amongst them, and the police would easily flush him out.

The only option was to go left. That way the canal would take him west, away from the town and into the countryside. Daniel would have to pass a few entrances accessible from housing estates and parks, but he would take that chance.

He started to run, took three strides and stopped.

On a bridge a car skidded to a halt, a black BMW. Daniel knew instantly that it would be a police officer and that he'd need to turn around and head into town.

Correct on both counts.

The officer's gaze fixed upon him. Daniel turned and powered along the canal towpath as the officer gave chase.

Flashes of blue cut through the hedgerows between the car park and waterway. There was another decision to make now as he ran alongside the locks. Did he run across the cobblestone footbridge and descend down the slate slope which ran underneath the ring road? Leave the canal via a break in the hedgerow and head back onto the ring road? Give himself up?

As his pursuers closed in, his breathing became rapid. He was panicking, and argued with himself as to what he should do next.

Then the world went crazy.

First, he felt arms wrap around his waist, then he hit the gravel and dust-covered ground. He took a blow to the head and the sirens stopped – not just the sirens but the nearby traffic, the people, the seagulls...every sound seemed to have been sucked into a vacuum. Only one remained: his blood pumping around his body.

Through squinted eyes, he saw two more police officers advance along the towpath. He struggled to free himself. He gave a kick, but it had no effect; his body was held too tight to the ground to achieve any force. Daniel's only saving grace was that the policeman was fumbling with his handcuffs.

He tried a second, third, and a fourth kick.

No good.

He pulled his knee as high as he could and pushed down hard. The pressure on his body suddenly released. A whimper was followed by a splash of water as the winded policeman fell backward into the still canal water.

There was a chance to get away and he took it; he forced his body up and ran.

The sound came flooding back.

Traffic. Five lanes of traffic just beyond a metal railing. It was busy, and he weighed up his options.

He had only one.

He needed to start running and not stop. Out here he was a sitting duck.

SIXTY-NINE

Rhodes and Murray drove at around fifty miles an hour as they advanced around the northern section of the ring road. The Audi slowed a little as it came to an island before accelerating away down the hill towards the retail park.

Murray's phone rang loudly. He answered it. "Hi, love."

"Now don't panic, but I'm at the hospital," his wife said.

Rhodes glanced across at his passenger, whose face had lost all colour.

"What?"

"I had a pain, so I thought I'd get it checked out. It seems I am in slow labour. It's happening, Joel – our little man's on his way."

"Oh shit!"

Rhodes flashed his headlights at an old brown car that struggled to move out of the way.

"Don't go driving like a maniac; they said it could be hours before anything happens. Joel, it's really happening – I love you so much. See you in a bit."

"Love you too. Bye."

Murray looked across at his boss.

He was forced back into his seat as Rhodes floored the pedal and the engine roared.

"Get on the phone, get a car and get to your wife!" Rhodes said.

Murray caught a glimpse of a figure sprinting along the roadside and straight through the traffic lights into the oncoming traffic.

"I'm just going catch that bastard first," he said as he jumped from the car.

Traffic slowed their progress. Murray leapt from the car and started to run. He only got two full car lengths away when his phone rang again. The sound distracted him, and seconds later his body was thrown upward onto the bonnet of an oncoming car.

SEVENTY

Daniel heard the breaks screech behind him and could hear a scream, but he wasn't stopping for anyone, nor was he going to look back.

He was back on the canal towpath headed south toward the Tesco part of town. New scenarios played out in his mind as he tried to work out how best to get away.

In the distance another police officer was running towards him. He left the towpath via a small set of steps and made his way across to the Weavers Wharf retail park.

The shops were open but, being Tuesday afternoon, footfall was low. This gave Daniel a free run into the town centre. The downside of this was there were very few people to blend in with. Ever more police officers appeared.

He ran through the shopping area, then stopped and glanced up at the grey structure in front of him. The Swan Centre multi-storey car park. He felt hollow.

He had a new plan. He wasn't a coward any more, and he'd found the ideal place to become an even braver man. You can only value life if you have a life to put a value to, he thought. The officers gained ground on him. He took one last look up at the building ahead.

Current value of my life – worthless, he thought as he started to run.

SEVENTY-ONE

Empty and silent, just what Daniel needed.

He stood with his face flush to the lift door. Taking deep breaths, his eyes tightly shut, he waited for the lift to stop.

"Floor two, doors opening."

Stepping free of the metal box, the brightness took time to adjust to; he moved slowly at first, then quickened his pace. Level two was empty. He strode up a ramp and found a few more cars on level three. There was some kind of 4x4 parked in the last bay. That would hide him for a while.

There was noise but around street level; nothing up here on the third level.

Daniel let out long heavy sobs; the realisation that his world was crumbling around him had finally overwhelmed him.

None of it seemed real.

He scanned the empty bays on this level, bays he'd often used himself.

He traced through the days, trying in desperation to figure out at what point it had all started to go wrong.

Sweating, breathless, being hunted down by the police. It was utterly insane!

His phone vibrated in his pocket.

'U ok X'

Daniel read the text message four times. His son may not have been Shakespeare, but no three words had ever before meant so much.

He rushed to reply – his thumb rattled across the buttons. He wanted to pour out his heart, to say, 'I'm sorry son, I know you're confused and don't want to talk, but you have to believe me, I did not kill your mom. I loved her with all my heart and, God, she hurt me, but I would never think of doing what they've said I did. You make me happy, you kept the smile on my face and all I wanted was for you to be happy in return. I know how much your mom means to you and that, if nothing else, is why I wouldn't do it. You know how much I love you, Ollie and I would never want to cause you that kind of pain. Things are going to be strange but I will work something out and the police will get it right and find the person who did this to your mom.'

Of course, he didn't write that. Instead he wrote:

'Are you? I did not do it – Love you'

There was a long pause, which seemed to last an eternity, then the reply.

'I no, I miss mom, miss u. Make it beta dad plz.'

'I will I promise'

'G2G, police ere x'

'love you, see you soon.'

This time, no reply. Daniel waited, willing some response. He read the entire message over and over. He flicked across his menu to his photos and scrolled through photos of Ollie. He was still looking at them when he heard the footsteps.

He didn't look up. He guessed it was one of two people: Tesar or Rhodes. Either way it meant trouble.

He raised his head. Rhodes was a few feet away, expressionless, his hands held down by his side like a gunslinger ready to duel.

"I see bad cop showed up; where's good cop?"

"Doesn't make any difference who turned up, all that matters is it's over."

"It's not over till we find Jakub Tesar."

"Not going to happen, Daniel."

Rhodes's reply shocked Daniel. What was he saying? It was almost as if they weren't even looking for Tesar.

"You don't believe me?"

It was a statement more than a question, but Rhodes answered it. Still a few feet away – not too close but not too far away either, if Stone tried something.

"It's not about believing, it's about proving."

"You're the police, for God's sake. Prove it then."

Rhodes didn't reply.

"Easier to arrest the weaker man, tie up all your loose ends, and get a pat on the back from your boss, is that it?"

"You play this so called *weak man* well, Daniel. I have a sergeant who may not walk again, and another colleague who will be throwing up canal water for a week, and all because of the *weaker* man."

Rhodes watched as Daniel pushed himself to his feet.

Stone had begun to scale the low wall around the edge of the car park level. Rhodes did some quick calculations. Shit. By the time he could pounce, Stone's face would be splattered across the pavement. He needed to think, and quickly.

"No, don't do it, Daniel." He tried to keep his tone friendly, talking to him the way his mother would have done. Avoid confrontation, his mind told him, which in these circumstances was pretty damn hard.

"Why, don't fancy another death on your conscience?"

"Now stop, before it kills you. You don't want that, do you?"

Daniel froze, he'd heard those words once before. That time, he'd been cowering in pain as Jakub Tesar towered above him.

One of them, he was a policeman – that's why they won't go find him, they've set me up. Daniel looked down. A crowd had gathered: police, ambulance staff, passersby, all staring up at him.

"Think of Ollie – his mother's dead, do you think he wants to see his dad dead too? He needs you, Daniel. You're all he's got."

Daniel turned his back on the police officer and sat down.

Rhodes was happy with the new position; it meant that if he made a move now there was more chance of saving Stone. He could grab him around the chest from behind and pull backwards.

"You have children, don't you, Rhodes?"

"What is it with people wanting to know about my daughter?"

"Do you remember the day she was born?"

"Of course."

"I still remember the day when Ollie entered the world. As I drove from the hospital it felt like the car was floating. There I was, thinking that people were all staring, wondering what it was like to be me. I felt like I was a celebrity. I believed most people would have swapped their life for mine that day. I was the only one who could feel it, the pride I'd felt holding my child, my son, in my arms. I stepped through the front door of my house, looking down at the single greatest achievement of my entire life. Those days are gone now."

Rhodes just watched him as he spoke, ready to react if a need arose.

"These people stare now, hoping to catch a glimpse of a man they fear, and you're to blame. You and your team. I've told you over and over – I didn't do any of this. My words don't seem to matter. You puffed out your chest like a silverback and warned the world that I was a monster. You want to cage me like a vicious animal, have me become the newest inductee in the murderer's hall of fame. My name written in gold next to the likes of West and Sutcliffe."

He stared at Rhodes; went to speak again. Instead, he wet his dry lips with his tongue and was silent.

"Great speech, Shakespeare – now, you want to hear mine? It's a little less full of crap and a lot more to the point."

Daniel didn't answer.

"Innocent men don't jump, so get down and prove me wrong, or jump and prove me right."

SEVENTY-TWO

Daniel had gotten down, trying to prove Rhodes wrong.

He was sitting in an interview room in Kidderminster police station. Rhodes was sitting opposite. Next to Rhodes was DS Jackie Roberts.

Daniel had a little help from a solicitor.

"This interview is being conducted in an interview room at Kidderminster police station and is being recorded both on audio and video."

Murray motioned with his hands to the recording machine and the cameras.

"This interview may be given in evidence if your case is brought to trial. At the end of the interview I will give you a notice telling you what will happen to the tapes and how you can obtain a copy. Do you understand?"

Daniel nodded.

"I need you to answer aloud for the benefit of the tape."

"Yes."

"Thank you. Okay, I make the time 5:35pm and the date is 24th April. My name is DI Patrick Rhodes and the other officer present is-" Rhodes pointed Roberts who identified herself. "Can you give us your full name and date of birth?" he asked Daniel.

"Daniel Ian Stone, 15, 08, 1978."

Rhodes continued. "Also present is-" He pointed to the solicitor who sat across from him.

"Miss Daisy Hutchinson-Smyth of Hillard and Klien Solicitors."

Rhodes shuffled a few pieces of paper and began. He read Daniel his rights and asked him if he understood them.

Daniel said that he did, but actually he didn't. He didn't understand any of it. This time two weeks ago he was sitting on a lilo floating in a figure of eight around a pool, preparing himself for a new job, a new start. A new life. Now he was in a cold grey box preparing to answer questions he had no real answers for. While all of this went through his head, the words in his son's text kept replaying. He started to lose control, started to tremble, to cry. He didn't want to show the police his anguish so forced the tears back.

"Can you explain to us what you think it means, then?"

Rhodes knew the caution was important and he needed to make sure that the suspect understood it. It was up to the police to explain it, not the solicitor. Ninety-nine percent of all the suspects Rhodes had previously arrested had told him they understood it, but when asked to explain it, they couldn't.

"Not really. I don't understand any of this. I did nothing wrong, I shouldn't be here!"

"Okay. We'll get to all that in a while, but just so we're in no doubt, I will explain the caution. We split it into three parts. The first part: 'you do not have to say anything' – what that means is that we're going to ask you some questions; if you want to answer them you can, if you don't want to, you don't have to. Second part: '…but it may harm your defence if you do not mention when questioned something that you later rely on in court' – what we're saying here is that if we ask you a question and you decide, for whatever reason, not to answer it, and later on the case goes to court and when you come up with an explanation, then the court may say well, why didn't he answer that when he was first asked at the police station? And they might not believe you as much as if you had answered it today. And the third part is, 'anything you do say may be given in evidence', and that means we record the interviews and if it goes to court and the court want to hear what was said they can listen to the tapes. Understood?"

"I suppose that makes sense."

"Mr. Stone, do you understand, yes or no?"

"Yes, yes, I understand."

"And do you understand why you have been arrested?"

Daniel felt his body spasm. They kept saying "arrested". He had no idea why that was. "No!" was his angry response.

"Okay, I will explain it again fully. You've been arrested on suspicion of the murder of Mr. Roger Mackenzie, and also on suspicion of the murder of Mrs. Natalie Gibbs. Do you understand the charges?"

Daniel nodded begrudgingly.

"For the purpose of the tape, Mr. Stone."

"Sorry – I do, yes."

"Firstly, I would like to make you fully aware that you have been ruled out of any involvement in the manslaughter of Miss Abbie Flynn. More evidence has come to light and we now believe that the only connection to this crime was that you were in the vicinity at the time."

Finally, a bit of good news.

Then, almost as if Rhodes could read Daniel's mind: "Now, to the bad news. Daniel Stone, can you please confirm your movements during the night of Friday 20th April between the hours of eight and ten thirty."

It didn't take long for Daniel to work out where he was, and what was coming next. "I was at the Glades Leisure Centre."

"Could you please confirm what you were doing there?"

"I took my son to see Roger Mackenzie – he's a big fan; he got some books signed."

"Did you speak to Mr. Mackenzie?"

"On that night, or in general?"

Rhodes caught the note of sarcasm. "On the said night."

"We spoke a little; we've been friends for years, but he was working, he was very busy."

"Did you argue?"

"About what?"

"I don't know, Mr. Stone, you tell us."

"No we didn't argue; we hardly spoke."

Roberts wrote something down.

"So, even though this man was part of a team that double-crossed you, hung you out to dry professionally, you held no grudge against him?"

"No."

"What did you do once the reading was over – did you return to the leisure centre in question?"

There was an instant response, no need to think about it. "No. I went straight home. My son was excited but tired. We camped in the garden that night."

Rhodes looked down at his paper then meet Daniel's gaze once more. "Camping. Nice. Can we be completely clear on the last question: at no point did you return to the leisure centre?"

"No."

"No, you can't be clear?"

"No – I did not go back in."

Jackie Roberts pulled out three A4 photographic images from a small folder. The first picture showed a man entering the leisure centre, the second pointed towards the door, to where the writer had been found. The final image showed a man as he walked away from the leisure centre.

"For the benefit of the tape, I am showing Mr. Stone a copy of an image lifted from the CCTV system at the Glades Leisure Centre, taken on the night in question. Could you please confirm what the image shows, Mr. Stone?"

Daniel glared at it for a while. It was him using the vending machine. They were twisting everything.

"It's me going to use the vending machine."

"Can you confirm the time in the left-hand corner?"

Daniel looked – it was hard. The print was small but legible.

"Nine thirty-five."

"Thank you. That's ten minutes after the centre was emptied – so, did you return or not, Mr. Stone?"

"Yes, but not like you mean! I went to get for sweets for my son, not to shoot Mr. Mackenzie."

"So you returned to the scene of the crime?"

Daniel Stone fell silent.

SEVENTY-THREE

Outside the police station, the streets were darkening as the night drew in. A few cars already had their beams on. The road was busy.

Nothing had changed inside the interview room, apart from the fact that all four occupants were hungry. The odd stomach rumble gave that away. Of them all, the solicitor looked the most uncomfortable; she was missing out on a dinner engagement with a man she intended to settle down with. She vigorously scribbled notes down to release the frustration.

Daniel went through the questions in his head.

Did they really believe he was capable of any of this? They must, otherwise they'd have given up on this charade hours ago. He watched the second hand on the clock tick away.

"When did you find out about your wife's affair, Mr. Stone?"

"It wasn't an affair; she met Tom Gibbs months after we split."

"Okay, let's try some quick-fire questions to see if we can get anywhere. Did you shoot Roger Mackenzie?"

"No."

"Did you shoot your ex-wife?"

"No!"

"Did you ram her with your car last night? It was picked up on numerous ANPR cameras across Shropshire and North Worcestershire."

"No!"

"In that case, do you know who *was* driving your car?"

The room went quiet.

"Mr. Stone, did you hear my question?"

"Yes. I think I do, but you won't believe me."

"Try me."

"I think it was Jakub Tesar. I think he stole my car and drove it, killed my wife and drove back."

"So we're back to this, are we?"

"It's the only answer."

"No, no it's not – you expect us to believe some foreign salesman, who, let me add, no-one apart from you has ever seen, killed two people whose only connection was to you."

"You saw what he did to me."

There was a brief moment of reflection from all parties.

Daniel still had visible injuries. There was no denying the pain he was still in. The swelling and bruising seemed worse today that it had Sunday.

"Actually, I didn't," said Rhodes, breaking the silence.

"Do you mean to say you're denying having seen this?" Daniel pointed to his face.

"I can see the injuries you've sustained, yes. As yet, I haven't ascertained the cause."

"Do you think I did it to myself?"

Even Roberts turned to her boss and gave him a look of confusion.

284

"I wasn't sure at first, so I got it checked out." Rhodes picked up a medical report. "Do you want to hear the outcome? Facial injuries and bruising to the cheek area that could have been caused by impact with a long blunt object."

Daniel felt his face. Ran his fingers across the swollen bones, the damaged skin.

"I can't remember, I blacked out with the pain."

"Possibly a bat, but when I found you, there was blood on the door frame. I think you may have tried to head-butt your attacker and missed. Does that sound plausible?"

Rhodes carried on reading through the medical report, in each instance giving Daniel two options. The option Daniel wanted to hear and the option he didn't. Each time the injury could have been self-inflicted.

Daniel was drowning fast – everything he was saying, they twisted, so much so that he was starting to doubt himself.

SEVENTY-FOUR

Round and round in circles. The same questions. The same answers. Seconds became minutes. Minutes became hours.

If the interrogation had been a car journey, right about now they'd be on the hard shoulder, in a broken-down vehicle, awaiting rescue.

Daniel had broken his silence about the reasons Tesar was after him to begin with. He'd explained, in detail, about the whole three bullet list. Rhodes had disregarded it all, described it as nothing more than an imaginative twist on the genie scenario in fairytales.

So they were all back to square one.

They'd asked him about his involvement in Roger Mackenzie's shooting. He denied any involvement. He couldn't deny being in the location at the same time, though.

They had questioned him about the death of his ex-wife. He'd denied being there. Evidence showed his car had been in both the location she had last been seen and the location her body was found.

He could only imagine what was going on in the outside world. He tried hard not to think about it. About Ollie. Did Ollie know he was here now? Had the police or Tom Gibbs informed his son that he had been arrested for killing Ollie's mother? There were too many questions. It was driving him mad.

Then Jakub Tesar's image came to him again.

"You have to get him, Detective Rhodes. Please, he will kill my son."

On the table sat two transparent evidence bags. They were sealed. One contained a gun, found on the back seat of Daniel Stone's abandoned car. The other contained a pair of men's shoes. These shoes had come into police possession within the last few hours, found in the lost luggage department at a local train station.

"Daniel, I will ask you once more. Do you recognise the two pieces of evidence I've shown you?"

Daniel shook his head. Not as an answer to the detective's question but in disbelief at their stubbornness. "I've told you lies, hidden things from you."

There was movement in every direction. Rhodes lent forward. Vilani planted her elbows on the desk. The solicitor fidgeted uncomfortably in her seat.

"I have seen both pieces of evidence before. Those are the shoes I lost the night that girl got attacked. That gun is the one Jakub Tesar threatened me with. But you know all this, don't you?"

"Have you ever touched this gun?"

Daniel shook his head again.

"For the benefit of the recording, Mr. Stone shook his head. So, would it shock you to find out that the only set of prints on this weapon, the gun used to kill both your ex-boss and your ex-wife, were yours?"

Daniel struggled to breath. His windpipe seemed to inadvertently fold in on itself. He felt a terrible pain in his stomach.

"You have a brother, am I right, Daniel?" The questioning seemed to change direction wildly, like a pinball.

There was another long pause as Daniel tried to regain his breath; he closed his eyes at this new question. When he opened them, Rhodes noticed the anger in his expression.

"Had."

"Had?"

"Yes, he died."

"Can you remember the circumstances of his death?"

"Why are you doing this to me?"

Rhodes leaned forward. "I'm just trying to do my job, Mr. Stone."

"My brother died of a bleed to the brain. He was attacked at a train station by some thugs. He died from his injuries, days later in hospital."

"Am I right in thinking you were also there that night?"

"Correct, I was also attacked."

"When I first met you, you told my colleague DS Joel Murray and I a very similar story about an attack at the train station. Do you remember?"

"Yes."

"Call me suspicious, Mr. Stone, which I am. Comes with the territory. What do you think the odds would be that a normal law-abiding citizen such as yourself would be attacked in exactly same way, in the same sort of location, and be saved by the same person twice?"

"No, my brother saved me the first time. Jakub Tesar saved me the second."

Rhodes got up from his chair. "And that is exactly why I don't believe I need to be looking for Mr. Jakub Tesar. Listen, I need a coffee, so I'm going to give you a chance to think. Use the time wisely – figure out why you're really sitting here."

"Interview terminated at 8:17pm," Jackie Roberts said.

The two detectives stood and left the room, followed by the solicitor.

Daniel was left alone with his thoughts.

SEVENTY-FIVE

Although it was late and most of the offices were empty, the CID room was full. Rhodes sat in the middle of the room. Vilani, Roberts, Crooks and Bates all sat a desk facing their boss. DCI Graham was also present, standing at the far end of the room with his back turned.

"What do you think?" asked Roberts.

"I think he's telling the truth. I'm going to take one last look at the CCTV from the station. It all started there, and I need to work out what it was."

"Stone had nothing to do with that," Graham offered.

"No, he didn't, but something happened that night that turned him into a killer, because, as far as I can see, he was fine before that."

Rhodes switched on his monitor and settled down for what he supposed might be a long night.

Bates's email pinged. It was the forensic team. He read the email to himself and then got everyone's attention. "I just got some details back on the gun. It's a CZ 75 semi-automatic pistol. It's made in the Czech Republic. Produced there since 1975."

"Tesar is from the Czech Republic," said Crooks.

"Widely distributed all over the world and used by the Czech police force. Just to make it a little more difficult to narrow down, it is by far the most popular model of firearm in the Czech Republic," Bates continued. "This specific gun was issued to a force in the Liberec region. I did another check and a certain Jake Carpenter served with British army for six months around this area."

Graham beamed; he'd put two and two together and made five again. "So, we finally have some evidence linking Tesar to this whole damn case," he said.

Patrick Rhodes looked up from his monitor. "It's not Jakub Tesar, and I'm about to find out why."

SEVENTY-SIX

Daniel didn't raise his head as the interview room door opened with a click, not even when this was followed by the scraping of the chair opposite him. He let out a heavy sigh; he was drained, confused, and the detectives were back with more questions. Questions he had no answers to, and even the answers he did have were not the ones they wanted. The answers he gave even he was starting to question.

He firmly massaged his eyes over the tops of his dry eyelids.

The sound of slow purposeful clapping and the sound of a familiar voice forced him to open his eyes.

"Congratulations, you're doing brilliantly. If you keep this act up they'll have no option other than to lock you up for a long time." The words came from the mouth of Jakub Tesar.

"You piece of shit," screamed Daniel as he jumped from his chair.

"Hey, calm down."

"I'll calm down when you're behind bars."

Three Bullets

"Never going to happen, fuckwit. I'm only here for a quick visit, I just need you to do something for me and I'll be off."

"You killed my wife…"

Tesar spun the bagged gun on the table in circles. "Think you'll find she's your *ex*-wife, in every sense of the word."

He took a pen and a piece of paper out of his pocket and pushed it across the table towards Daniel. "I'm here for that final name, and then it all goes away. You see, you started this, and all you need to do is give me that name and you can finish it. I have one last bullet."

"This is never going away. I don't know how you've set me up, but I will find out and get you."

"Daniel, you will rot in prison before you ever find out where I am. Now sit down, shut up and listen. The name – it's important. Shall I offer you some suggestions? I would have said that girl in the hospital – shame her parents beat you to that one though. What about that footballer bloke your dead wife was shagging? Bet that hurt, thinking about him on top of the love of your life every night. I've seen her and man, you punched way above your weight there. We had sex before I killed her; I say before, it may have been after – it all happened so fast."

Deep in his stomach Daniel felt repulsion and anger. "You sick piece of shit!"

"I'll take that as a no. What about yourself? Take that gun and do it. Go on, your son will thank you for it."

This was too much. Daniel knew the gun wasn't loaded; Tesar was just taunting him. Daniel just wanted to hit him, hit him hard, so hard that he would never got up.

"You leave my son out of this."

"You're the one that got him involved, Daniel; you wrote his mother's name down on that piece of paper. Now the poor lad has a corpse for a mum and a murderer for a dad; I have seen some dysfunctional families in my time, but yours is pretty fucked up."

Tesar was enjoying every second of this. He could feel Daniel Stone's anger intensify. He carried on pushing. "Even the pigs want you to do it, that's why they've left the gun on the fucking table. I pictured it happening just like this, that's why I had to get you to take your shoes off on the train. Once they'd been found they became evidence against you. I just can't believe they never noticed you had no shoes on when you got off the train. The shoes are a vital part, the timing of when they found them, even more so. Too soon, and they would find the bullet before I could get to you. Too late and my plan would be over. You see, the final bullet needed to somehow to be placed in this room without me having to bring it in at the exact same time you got arrested. The third bullet is in the heel of the right shoe – take a look. Even I'm a little amazed by how easy it's been."

"Why?"

Tesar had talked so long that Daniel's anger had gone. There was no need for self-pity. He needed to figure this out.

"Why not? I spent years making sure it was the right time. The train wasn't the first time we'd met – it was years back, just after your brother died. You must remember – you seemed to shut off for a while, shut everyone out. I got very close to you and your wife.

"You don't remember? You should have asked Natalie; she would remember me. You shut her out. Your brother's death nearly finished your marriage then. I think me being around contributed to more doubt in her mind – she saw what a proper man could do and she wanted more than what Daniel Stone had to offer. I suppose I planted a seed in more ways than one. How is Ollie, by the way?"

There was a pause.

"Just do it. Finish yourself off; get rid of another one of the world's useless fucking runts. But first, have a moment to think something over – Ollie was born ten months after your brother's death, so he was conceived in that dark period where you barely uttered two words to each other. Tell me this, Daniel – can you honestly remember making love to your wife at that time?"

Then Tesar got what he wanted. Daniel Stone snapped. "Shut up, shut up, shut the fuck up!"

Daniel had stood up, unaware that in his right hand he held the gun.

"Yes, Daniel, that's what we need, anger! Let it out – pick a name, or do yourself."

"You're not going to get away with this."

"I already have. You've had them chasing their tails all along, looking for me in all the wrong places. They'll work it all out in the end, but by that time you'll be locked up for good."

Tesar gradually raised himself from his chair.

"Sit down!" Daniel pushed Tesar back into the seat so hard that the thin metal legs buckled.

Daniel Stone turned the gun on Tesar.

"Now you're waving a gun at me that's not even loaded. One moment, here, look."

He took the gun out of Daniel's hand and swivelled it so it pointed down; he then picked up the right shoe and forced the heel to the left. Daniel watched as the leather

295

heel slipped effortlessly away from the sole. The third bullet sparkled in the light.

"One last bullet. One last pull of this trigger and it all goes away." Tesar loaded the gun and handed it to Stone, who tried to steady his trembling hand. He pointed the gun directly at Jakub Tesar.

"If I shoot you, then they'll have you at last!"

"To them I will just be another victim of your deranged madness."

"Not if I shoot you in the leg."

"They'll work all this out. They will put two and two together; it's their job. That Rhodes guy has been a little slow, but I have faith in him. He will work it out. Your shoes needed to be here to hold the bullet at the right time. They haven't tested them yet."

Daniel pounced forward; Jakub leapt from his chair. As Daniel's finger squeezed the trigger, Jakub took hold of the nozzle and forced it downward.

A single bullet fired. The sound echoed. There was a brief silence, followed by stomach-churning screams of pain.

SEVENTY-SEVEN

The footage from the railway station played on Rhodes's screen again. He felt as though he'd been there that night, he'd watched this scene so many times.

There was a hum coming out of Bates's computer. He was searching for his own answers.

But Rhodes had figured it out. There was no great display of pride, though; he was too disappointed that it had taken so long.

He was getting old. He was losing his touch.

It wasn't the words Stone had used; it had been the movements he made that finally gave it all away.

"I know who the killer is. All along it's been staring us in the face."

The team gathered to hear Rhodes explain.

"Ask yourself a question – who is he talking to?"

They all watched the footage on the monitor.

"Drunken people like to talk to themselves, and he was pretty drunk," said Bates.

"But not like that – look at him. He's holding eye contact; he is deep in conversation with someone."

DCI John Graham straightened up. "You're not going to tell me you believe there's some ghost or something doing this?"

Rhodes thought about what he was going to say a few times in own head. He worked the scenario through from his point of view. Then he put himself in Daniel Stone's shoes, or lack of shoes, to be more precise.

"Not a chance, but I think I might be able shed some light on who it was. Bates, Google Tesar and see what it means. I think we may be somewhat surprised. There is more to the shoes as well, look – I missed it before, but he's barefoot when he leaves the train. Something happened on that train, something that meant he tried to get rid of them. We need them tested – they hold more clues than we think."

"He's pissed up, Rhodes – we're lucky he's got his trousers on," added a more frustrated Graham.

"No, the shoes were left for a reason. That's the part I'm not a hundred percent sure of."

Bates clicked away on his keyboard, "Boss."

"Yes, Bates."

"Tesar is an old Czech name for a man who works with wood, like a carpenter."

"Exactly, like a carpenter. An English translation could be Jacob Carpenter or maybe Jake Carpenter."

"His brother," said Roberts.

"His dead brother. I'm not going to sit here and let you make a mockery of this department, Rhodes. You're trying to say that this is down to a man who died over a decade ago?" Graham stormed off and took up his usual position near the window.

"Daniel Stone *did* kill Roger Mackenzie and Natalie Gibbs. You know what DID is, Sir?" he replied.

"It's a three-letter word, a past tense for do. Other than that, no," said Graham.

"Dissociative identity disorder. DID."

There was a look of disgust on the DCI's face.

The other officers got comfortable. This had become a spectator sport. A battle of wits. Graham had power on his side, while Rhodes had experience.

"No, I'm not swallowing this bullshit," said Graham, still gazing out of the window.

"It's a psychiatric condition. Most people would call it 'split personality'. Someone with DID symptoms display multiple distinct identities or personalities. Each split has its own behavioral pattern and outlook on interacting with the world around them."

"So, now Stone is a psycho."

"Maybe he always has been – or, at least, since the attack that killed his brother. I'll read on, shall I? The awareness and memory of a traumatic event are split off to survive in a relationship; in Stone's case, with his wife. The memories and feelings go into the subconscious part of the brain. These are experienced later as a separate personality. The process can happen repeatedly at different times so that new personalities develop. Each new personality can perform different functions that are either a help or a hindrance. Dissociation is a coping mechanism when faced with further stressful situations. Sound like anyone we know, Graham?"

Rhodes clicked off his computer and picked up his file. He motioned to DS Roberts that they were ready to re-question Daniel Stone.

The door burst open. A uniformed officer rushed in.

"Inspector Rhodes, you have a Daniel Stone in custody at present."

"Yes, why?"

"I heard shouting, so I took a look. There is a gun in there."

"It's okay, it's not loaded."

"That's what I was expecting you to say. You need to come and see this."

SEVENTY-EIGHT

Four detectives burst into the room: Rhodes, Graham, Bates and Vilani. In front of them on the floor lay Daniel Stone. He gripped his thigh hard as fountains of blood spurted from between his clenched fingers; with every beat of his heart more blood was released onto the cold grey floor. Daniel cried Jakub Tesar's name over and over.

Rhodes dropped to Daniel's side. "I told you I had the right man, and I told you I would prove it." Then he stopped talking.

There was fear in Daniel's eyes. He was almost childlike.

"I don't understand. I meant to shoot him, just to injure him enough. Just enough so you could see he was real, so you knew I wasn't lying. I was shaking. I must have lost control and shot myself. Did you get him?"

There was exchange of glances between the detectives, before Vilani made a phone call gesture. Rhodes nodded, and she disappeared back out the door.

"It's going to be okay; an ambulance is on its way. I'll let Ollie know you're okay."

"You got him, then? Please tell me you got Jakub Tesar."

"Yeah, we have him; we have him right here in the station."

The detective rose to his feet, nodding an 'I told you so' at DCI Graham.

"Hes going to end up in a hospital rather than a prison," said Graham.

"As long as he's off the streets, I don't give a shit where he is," Rhodes retorted.

*

Rhodes sat alone at his desk for a while, his head buried in his hands. Minutes passed before he worked out exactly what to tell Daniel Stone's son. He drew a deep breath and finally made the call he really didn't want to make.

SEVENTY-NINE

In the peaceful surroundings of St Matthew's Cemetery stood a lone man at the side of the meticulous manicured lawn, a single red rose in his hand. Dressed in a dowdy grey suit, he bent to kneel next to a mound of dirt that lay atop a freshly-covered grave, a bunch of rain drenched lilies decorating the centre of the dirt. The sodden and frayed ends of his trousers hung above worn boots. The right sleeve of the suit hung loose to one side, his right arm held underneath the breast of the suit in a sling.

"I've not come to say I'm sorry; in fact, I'm pretty damn happy you've finally gone."

The branches of a weeping willow dragged across the top of some ageing headstones resting against a crumbling stone wall. From the top of one came a magpie's cackle: one for sorrow. No second for joy, not here, not today.

The man brushed his wet fringe from his eyes. "You've always been shit at taking care of me. Now you're dead, see if you can give it a go. They'll never really know what I planned for that girl, so attractive and my God, what an arse. Dying got her off the hook, that's for sure. It would have been a thing of beauty if that dick hadn't run her over."

The man shuffled his hand around in his pocket before taking one final look around the graveyard and up toward the windows of the new-build semis that backed onto the cemetery.

Through the greyness of the day a silver charm bracelet shone, adorned with five or six charms, the centre one being a golden letter A.

"Look after this for me; take it with you and make sure it never finds the surface."

Using his good arm, the man buried the bracelet deep in the dirt, using his hand to dig until the hole was elbow deep. He covered the hole and got to his feet.

Lifting his head in a slow deliberate movement and raising it towards the sky, he poked out his tongue and let the rain splash into his mouth. Colin Templeton turned from the grave of his mother and smiled.

"Goodbye. I hope they give you hell wherever you go."

Colin strolled away from the cemetery and opened the door of his taxi. The windscreen wipers forced the excess water from the glass only to be called back into action as the screen was covered once more.

Colin turned the key, pulled away, and indicated onto the busy main road. He grinned. He was alone and happy.

His grin disappeared as three police cars blocked his path, sirens blaring, lights flashing.

He watched as DI Rhodes strode towards him and opened his door.

"Hi Colin, how's the arm?" He smiled as he pulled the man from the car by the material that held the sling around his neck.

"I think we need a chat, don't you? Did you really think I wouldn't catch you? For the record, I didn't get the DCI's job because I'm too good for it. I've just turned it down for a third time."

Rhodes smiled and held a charm bracelet in front of Templeton's watering eyes. It was covered in dirt. Templeton recognised it straight away, and he sank to the floor.

Rhodes reeled off the caution before dragging his yelping suspect to the second of the three cars.

EIGHTY

Rhodes removed his seat belt and left the car.

He looked up at the building before him: depressing. No matter how they painted a sunny picture of this place on their website, in reality it was four brick walls thrown together to house mad people. They hadn't even been bothered to keep the grounds tidy; flowerbeds ran wild with weeds.

Inside were people whose minds had failed them. People like Daniel Stone. Outside, it looked as though the world had given up on them, refused to admit that they existed.

There were better things he could be doing on a Sunday, especially a Sunday away from work. But Rhodes wanted to know something. So he'd made an appointment with the hospital manager and here he was.

The visit started out badly. Across the car park there was a BMW. And next to the BMW, Tom Gibbs.

This meant one thing. Ollie Stone was inside, visiting his father.

Rhodes took the lift to the third floor and waited outside the manager's office. As if by some evil conspiracy, Ollie

Stone was sitting two chairs down from him as he waited. Ollie looked older than he had the last time Rhodes had seen him, just over seven months ago. No longer a child, he was a young man, all pimples and fledgling facial hair.

Ollie looked up and looked away. Then he spoke. "You're the policeman that arrested my dad, aren't you?"

Rhodes just nodded.

"Thank you," said Ollie.

"For what?" Rhodes was puzzled.

The kid looked to be thinking. "I asked you to check on my dad. Remember, outside my house?"

Rhodes nodded silently again.

"You did. You saved his life. Seems there was someone trying to kill him after all. Just that it was a man in his own head. Freaky, hey?"

At that point the hospital manager Dr Sheridan Pemberton called Rhodes into his office. The office was filled with personal photos and art. There was a medical bed in the corner and the obligatory eye chart on the wall. Rhodes scanned down it in a fast motion. He got them all correct.

"How is he?" Rhodes asked. Dr Pemberton looked down at the paperwork in front of him.

"Inspector Rhodes, in the six months he's been a patient of ours, he's been the most delightful of men."

He paused.

"Ninety percent of the time, and then bam! He slips into this Jakub character and all hell breaks loose. He broke two security guards' noses last month, but, honestly, he is one of our better patients."

"Any chance of him being released?"

"About as much chance as me hooking up with one of my young nurses for a night."

"That bad, eh?"

The two men laughed.

"What about his son, how often does he visit? I just saw him outside."

"Every Sunday, and they sit and chat for hours. It really is a wonderful sight, unconditional love. It's actually quite heartbreaking when the boy leaves."

"Daniel ever cause any trouble while his son's around?"

"Not a bit. In fact, he lies in his room."

"Doing what?"

"I would expect mostly replaying his life with his son; you can go view him yourself if you wish."

Rhodes took some small offense to this comment. He hadn't come here to gloat, or to be a voyeur. "No thanks, this is a hospital, Doctor Pemberton, not a zoo. Just wanted to see if he was doing okay."

The doctor closed his notes. "Very well."

The two men rose from their chairs and shook hands. Rhodes made his way to the door but stopped as he turned the handle. "Just out of curiosity, what are his chances of ever getting out of this place?"

"The brain is a very powerful tool, Inspector, but when something goes wrong it can lead to utter destruction. There is a possibility that Daniel could get better, but Jakub will always be somewhere in his mind – and would you want Jakub Tesar out on the streets again?"

EIGHTY-ONE

The room was white. The plaster, the bed sheets, the curtains, all white; not clean, just white. There was mould breaking out from the far corner of the ceiling to the left of a toughened-glass window. An abundance of cracks branched out across the plaster.

Daniel Stone sat on the edge of the bed looking at his reflection in a Perspex mirror on the wall opposite. The Perspex reflected a distorted image back to him that he didn't recognise. The eyes staring back at him looked evil. What should have been the whites were a dark pink hue, almost red, and underneath his eyes was dark shadow. He was tired. Tired of the horrid dreams, tired of being alive.

The room was tidy. The bed was made, not a crease, not a single fold or line. Over the past five weeks Daniel's daily routine was taken up by an internal battle with boredom. He hated the TV room, it was full of nutters, so, making the bed was now a highlight of his day, and he revelled in how good he'd become at it.

He made no friends and his only enjoyment was seeing his son, whose photo hung on the wall near his bed. Today, even that couldn't raise a smile.

"Mr. Stone? Mr. Stone? Your medication," came a voice in the doorway.

Daniel didn't answer.

"Mr. Stone, I have your medication!"

There was still no movement. Then Daniel started to mumble. "Yesterday upon the stair, I met a man who wasn't there. He wasn't there again today. I wish, I wish, he'd go away..."

"Mr. Stone..."

Daniel turned and he glared at the gaunt, blonde-haired man who stood in front of him, leaning against the door frame.

"I'm sorry, Stuart, Mr. Stone isn't here today," Daniel turned to the mirror, and the corners of his lips rose to a sneer as he whispered: "Mr. Stone is dead."

Coming in 2014, the new Patrick Rhodes thriller...

False Hope
Gavin Jones

ONE

Mark Cavendish could see what was about to unfold, right there in the bar of his pub. He didn't know exactly how the mayhem would start, but he did know that there was only one outcome. He was so clear on this that he'd already called an ambulance. The last thirty minutes had been building up to this. Powerless, Cavendish leaned against the taps and watched, fully prepared for the fallout.

To his left, a group of seven girls, all in their early twenties, all with too much make-up and too few clothes on. They were out for a good night, enjoying the music and the atmosphere. This group was Cavendish's first problem.

The real problem was the loudest member; she was around five-foot-six, one of those girls who are told she's sexy by people who want to sleep with her, and actually believes them. This gave her a confidence that she really shouldn't have had. She was knocking back shots like they were about to become extinct. Not yet drunk enough to forget it was her twenty-first birthday, but drunk enough not to notice that her constant announcement of the fact was irritating other customers.

One of those customers, to the right of the landlord, was his second problem. He was sitting in the middle of five men all wearing dark designer suits. Jay O'Connor, thirty-nine years old, six-foot-three and just over fourteen stone of muscle. If the birthday girl was the fuel, this man was definitely the spark that would bring your house to the ground. Cavendish knew this for one reason: until eight years ago he was his boss. They owned a security firm, nightclubs, and protection, amongst other things. These other things were the reason Cavendish got out, but now O'Connor had come looking for a favour.

The pub was filled with the sound of cackling and the girl shouting, "It's my birthday today."

The spark was thrown, and the match was lit.

O'Connor rose from his seat and ambled across the lounge, snatching three darts from a man about to throw them at the board.

"Hey!"

O'Connor took no notice. One of his group dealt swiftly with the dart player, slamming his head against a table.

"Sorry if I'm being nosy, but I couldn't help overhearing that it's one of you lovely girls' birthday," he said, addressing the entire group.

The drunken girl smiled up at this handsome man in front of her. "That's me! You here to give me my present, sexy?"

He looked at her face and almost felt sorry for her for a second, then she prodded her friend and cackled again.

"Yes, I am. Happy birthday."

With that he slammed the three darts, point down, into the top of her head.

The pub erupted – her friends screamed and two men raced across to get to O'Connor; they didn't reach him, but were stopped in the tracks by heavy blows from two of the suited men. They fell hard against the floor.

Mark Cavendish shook his head and, for the first time in thirty minutes, walked around to the paying side of the bar. Three of the girls were shouting in his face for him to throw Jay O'Connor out. He took little notice; he bent down next to the table were the birthday girl was, looked into her closing eyes and sighed.

"There's an ambulance on its way. Now get her out of my pub, and fast. She'll be okay if you keep pressure on the wound."

He stood up and faced O'Connor. "Seriously, was there any need for that?"

"Do you remember the last time I came up to the bar? I warned you then."

"You said she was a bit loud."

"You've been out of the game for too long. You've forgot the lingo."

"I've forgot nothing, Jay. If you remember, I taught you."

"Times have moved on, my friend. You didn't pussy about like they just did in your day. Let's see how good your memory is. I want Patrick Rhodes's home address, Cav, I want his wife's car reg, and I want to know where his daughter studies. You have till 8am tomorrow or mopping that bitch's blood up will be the least of your worries."

With that, the five men left, got into a black BMW and drove away, leaving behind them the sound of girls screaming and sirens wailing.

TWO

For once, Patrick Rhodes could see the wooden top of his desk. His files were neatly stacked on the floor. His keyboard was pushed close to the monitor and all his pens stood upright in a plastic desk tidy.

He switched off his light and closed the office door. Across the office, dressed in a dark green trouser suit, sat a female detective. Her shoulder length ginger hair was loose against her neck. She looked up at her boss.

"Have a good time, Patrick," said DS Jackie Roberts.

He gave a sheepish smile, loosened his silver tie and unfastened his top button.

"Hey, you never know, old man, you might really enjoy the flight," she chuckled.

"Don't say that word, please, Jackie."

Despite standing just shy of six-foot-three and weighing a pound or two under fourteen stone, the mere mention of the words flight or plane sent his knees to jelly.

He forced a fake laugh and he made his way to the door. As he descended the stairs, he phoned his wife. She answered on the second ring.

"Hi love, you okay?"

"Yeah, on my way to get Sadie. She can't believe that this time tomorrow she'll be going on holiday abroad with her father for the first time ever. You'd think she was a child, not twenty."

"I really should have done it years ago – I'm sorry. What time will you be back?"

Rhodes opened the door and made his way across the staff car park to his silver Audi A5.

"Not sure – elevenish, we'll probably stop off for some food."

"Okay, see you later – love you."

"Love you too."

Rhodes got into his car and left the police station, little knowing that this would be the last time he left that car park as a policeman.

*

Rita Rhodes slowed her car down to around ten miles per hour. She glanced left and right along the wide road, checking for a parking space. There were none. She would double back around and try again. There was a constant stream of people leaving the university, so at some point a space would become free.

On her third loop a Black BMW indicated right and pulled out. She indicated into the empty space; the entrance to her daughter's university was directly to her right.

Even with the extra loops she was still a little early. The traffic on the way up had been clear. She made herself comfortable in her seat and dozed for a while.

The street she'd stopped in was wide and so were the pavements; they had grass verges in between the boundaries of the houses and the kerb. Here and there a horse chestnut tree cast shadows across the street.

Behind Rita the same black BMW that had moved so she could park was manoeuvering into a freshly vacant space three cars back. In the passenger seat sat Jay O'Connor, his eyes trained on the entrance of the university.

"We'll wait until she's in, okay? They'll stop at some point for food. That's when you take them. Once they're in the car, call me and I'll make the call to Rhodes. He's about to wish he'd never crossed the O'Connor family, that's for sure."

O'Connor slipped out of the passenger door. He took a slow walk down the residential street. Most of the houses were late -Victorian style, semi-detached, now mostly converted into student digs.

He smiled into Rita Rhodes's window as he walked past. He had plans for her.